"Do you want to talk about what happened?"

"There were loud noises and smoke and darkness, children screaming, blood..." Deni said. "I thought we were all going to die."

"You're okay now," Ryan said softly.

"All day I had flashes of déjà vu. I think it was the mock bus wreck I participated in. Was it like that for you, too?"

"It's so different in a real emergency. It was dark. There was a lot of debris. We weren't sure where everyone was."

"Right away I heard people say it was a bomb."

"No one is saying yet exactly what caused the explosion. They probably don't know yet."

"Do you mean it might not be a bomb at all?"

"I don't know."

The sob that escaped her startled her. She her mouth with both hands. tears flowed freely. Rya again. "It's okay," he s

She shook her head. It- not okay, but she appreciate comfort her.

MOUNTAIN TERROR

Cindi Myers

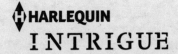

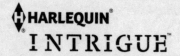

INTRIGUE™

ISBN-13: 978-1-335-58236-2

Recycling programs
for this product may
not exist in your area.

Mountain Terror

Copyright © 2022 by Cynthia Myers

For questions and comments about the quality of this book,
please contact us at CustomerService@Harlequin.com.

Harlequin Enterprises ULC
22 Adelaide St. West, 41st Floor
Toronto, Ontario M5H 4E3, Canada
www.Harlequin.com

Printed in U.S.A.

Cindi Myers is the author of more than fifty novels. When she's not plotting new romance story lines, she enjoys skiing, gardening, cooking, crafting and daydreaming. A lover of small-town life, she lives with her husband and two spoiled dogs in the Colorado mountains.

Books by Cindi Myers

Harlequin Intrigue

Eagle Mountain Search and Rescue

Eagle Mountain: Search for Suspects

The Ranger Brigade: Rocky Mountain Manhunt

Eagle Mountain Murder Mystery: Winter Storm Wedding

Visit the Author Profile page at Harlequin.com.

CAST OF CHARACTERS

Deni Traynor—She thought when her widowed father moved to Eagle Mountain they would be closer than ever, but now that he has disappeared, she's learning how much she doesn't know about her dad.

Ryan Welch—The climber and SAR volunteer has been attracted to Deni since they first met in the local coffee shop, but is he ready for a new relationship that involves so many complications, including a woman whose father might be a terrorist?

Mike Traynor—The former truck driver is known for protesting local development, but has he turned to violence to make his point?

Agents Olivera and Ferris—The agents from the US Bureau of Alcohol, Tobacco, Firearms and Explosives seem to have the idea that Deni and her father are working together to set these bombs. What do they know that she doesn't?

"Al"—Mike Traynor's mysterious new friend seems to have disappeared along with Mike. What are the two up to?

Chapter One

The school bus lay on its side halfway down the canyon,
its path from the roadway marked by the torn limbs of
trees and deep groove marks in the layer of snow over
the rocky surface. As Ryan Welch and the other members of Eagle Mountain Search and Rescue made their
way down to the wreck, the terrified screams of children rose above the roar of rushing waters from the
creek below. An involuntary shiver raced up Ryan's
spine, and he picked up the pace, half skidding down
the incline, his boots sinking into the snow with every
step, the vacuum mattress strapped to his back bounc-
ing against his pack.

"We've got to secure the vehicle before we can go inside," SAR Captain Tony Meisner ordered. He directed
a trio of volunteers—Ted Carruthers, Eldon Ramsey
and Austen Morrissey—to affix lines to the vehicle
and chock the wheels, while the others waited in an
anxious huddle just up the slope.

The screaming in the vehicle rose to a fever pitch,
and several children stuck their heads out the open
windows of the bus. "Help!" they screamed, and waved

their hands, frantic. "Our teacher is hurt and I think the bus driver is dead!" one girl shouted.

"Remain calm!" Tony, a tall, bearded man in his late thirties, instructed through a handheld hailer. "Help is on the way."

"That bus isn't going anywhere now." Ted Carruthers, tall and wiry, with thick gray hair and a gray goatee, reported to Tony. "It's wedged against some good-sized boulders, and we've secured all the lines."

Tony nodded and studied the vehicle. "Let's see if we can get those back emergency doors open and go in that way," he said. "If not, we'll climb on top."

Tony led the way to the bus. "Can someone open the emergency exit?" he shouted.

"I'll try," a voice called from inside. Ryan couldn't tell if the speaker was an adult, or an older child. The person who had called in the accident hadn't been able to tell the dispatcher how many people were on the bus, only that it was full of middle school students and their chaperones, on their way home to Eagle Mountain, Colorado, from a drama competition on the other side of the pass.

The back door of the bus popped open and children began to spill out. "Stop!" Tony shouted. "Nobody move!"

Everyone froze. One boy had one foot on top of a boulder beside the bus, the other still inside the vehicle, but he stilled and looked expectantly at the SAR commander. "You're going to exit one at a time," Tony instructed. "A volunteer will help each of you and check you out to make sure you're okay. Then another volunteer will escort you to the road. If you're hurt, remain inside the bus until one of us can help you. Understood?"

Choruses of "Yes," and "Okay" and "Yes, sir," rose from the bus.

Things moved quickly after that. Sheriff's deputies and fire department personnel moved in to assist the children who hadn't been injured. As soon as they were out of the way, Ryan, along with paramedic Hannah Richards and nurse Danny Irwin, climbed into the bus, scrambling awkwardly over the seats to reach the huddle of people near the middle.

While Hannah and Danny focused on a child who was screaming and clutching her arm, Ryan moved toward a woman who sat slumped against the roof of the sideways bus. Blood poured from a gash on her head. Twentysomething, with honey-brown hair now soaked in blood, she wore a stick-on name badge that identified her as Ms. Traynor. "Ma'am?" Ryan touched her cheek, which was soft and reassuringly warm, in spite of the chill that had seeped into the bus. "Ma'am, can you hear me?"

The woman's eyelids fluttered, then she looked up at him with green-blue eyes. Beautiful eyes, which should have been full of distress, considering her situation. Instead, she began to giggle.

Ryan sat back on his heels. "Deni! You're supposed to be seriously injured. You're not supposed to laugh."

"I know!" She choked back a fresh wave of laughter, and tried to sit up a little straighter against the sloping roof. "It just sounds so funny when you call me *ma'am*."

"Could you just get back in character, please?"

She assumed a sober expression. "Of course. Where were we?"

"I'm trying to assess if you're conscious or not."

"Right." She closed her eyes and rested her head back against the bus once more. The high school student who had volunteered to do the makeup for this training exercise had done a phenomenal job, making Deni's injuries look real. The only thing missing, he realized, was the metallic smell of blood. Instead, the aroma was slightly sweet. He forced his thoughts back to the task at hand. His job was to assess Deni's status.

But as soon as he touched her shoulder, she opened her eyes again. "Am I conscious or not?" she asked. "I can't remember."

Before he could answer, Danny leaned over Ryan's shoulder. "What have we got here?" he asked.

Ryan decided to skip ahead in the script. "We have a young woman with a head injury. She's conscious, pupils evenly dilated and responsive to light, vision tracking." He reached up and gently felt the back of her head. "No depression of the skull." He caught and held Deni's gaze. "Have you vomited?"

She wrinkled her nose. "No!"

Ryan shifted his hand to her neck. "Pulse is strong and regular," he said, ignoring the flutter of awareness at the feel of her warm, silken skin against his fingers. "Are you hurt anywhere else?" he asked.

"No. I was in my seat, with the seat belt fastened, when the bus went off the road, and I was slammed against the side of the bus and hit my head." She touched the gash on her forehead and winced, convincingly, then stared at her hand, now red and sticky with fake blood.

"Let's get her in a cervical collar and on the litter for transport to the ambulance," Danny said.

"What am I supposed to do now?" Deni whispered after Danny had left them.

"Whatever we tell you," Ryan said.

"That could get pretty interesting," she said. The words—and the flirtatious look that accompanied them—sent a rush of heat through him. Maybe she really had hit her head—this was a side of Deni he hadn't seen before in their frequent encounters at the local coffee shop where they both stopped before work most mornings. Not that he knew her well, but he had definitely noticed her. He looked forward to seeing her. He had even been thinking about working up the nerve to ask her out.

Tony and Eldon moved in with the litter and the three of them set about the awkward task of balancing it over the bus seats and helping Deni into it. She played the part of a disoriented injured person well, complete with being uncooperative and unable to follow directions. "You don't have to be quite this realistic," Ryan whispered to her ten minutes into the ordeal. "We have other patients to see to."

"Sorry," she mumbled, and meekly hoisted herself onto the litter.

He left Eldon and Tony to transport her to the roadway, while he moved on to the next "victim," a thirteen-year-old boy who sported an impressive network of cuts on his face, as well as bruises indicating a broken nose.

He moaned dramatically as Ryan touched him. "Am I going to be scarred for life?" he asked.

"It's amazing what plastic surgery can do," Ryan said. "Can you tell me where it hurts?"

"My back hurts."

"Your back?" Maybe the dramatic makeup job on the kid's face was designed to throw him off. "Where exactly, does it hurt?"

The boy started to sit up, but Ryan pushed him down. "It's very important for you to lie still. If you try to move, you could injure yourself further. Just tell me where the pain is."

"It's in the middle of my back," the boy said.

Ryan prodded the boy's ankle. "Can you feel that?" Each victim had been coached ahead of time as to what symptoms they should display, but the first responders had been kept in the dark about what to expect.

"I can feel you fine." The boy sat up. "I just ended up laying on something and it's poking me."

Ryan reached back and retrieved a red aluminum water bottle. The boy's face lit up. "Hey, I've been looking for that."

"Great," Ryan said. "Now could you lie back down and let me treat you?"

The boy grinned. "Sure." He lay back down and let out another moan. "My face! My modeling career is ruined!"

DENI, FREED FROM the litter, some of the corn-syrup-and-food-coloring fake blood wiped away, sat on a boulder just past the ambulance, her hands wrapped around a mug of coffee. The trip up from the canyon, strapped to the litter, had been more frightening than she had thought it would be, though the search and rescue volunteers had assured her they knew what they were doing and wouldn't drop her. Still, the sensation of having to rely totally on other people for her safety had been unsettling.

Those few minutes with Ryan in the bus had been fun, though. She smiled, remembering. After weeks of exchanging hellos and comments about the weather with the good-looking man who always stopped for coffee about the same time she did, it had been nice to get a little more up-close and personal, as it were. Careful questioning of friends who kept track of that kind of thing had revealed that Ryan Welch was twenty-four, worked for the Ride Brothers, a local manufacturer of snowboards and skateboards, and was not, as far as anyone knew, seriously dating.

As it so happened, neither was she. So the challenge became how to arrange for the two of them to go out together. She could simply ask, she supposed, but if he turned her down it would be too embarrassing. So her plan was to let him know she was interested and take it from there.

"More coffee?" Iris Desmet, owner of the Cake Walk Café, approached, a large insulated carafe in one hand.

"I'm good." Deni smiled. "Thanks for providing refreshments."

"It's the least I can do. Would you like a cookie?" Iris slipped her hand into the pocket of her apron and pulled out a large cookie wrapped in Cling Wrap. "Choco-late chip."

"Wow. Thank you." Deni accepted the cookie, which she knew from previous experience was as close to per-fect as a cookie could get.

"How's your dad?" Iris asked. "He usually comes in a few times a week, and I haven't seen him for a while."

"Oh, he's fine. Just busy, I guess." She struggled to keep her smile in place, and tried to ignore the sudden cramping in her stomach. The truth was, she hadn't seen her dad in several days, either. She had spoken to him on the phone, once, when he called to tell her he was going to be working on something for the next few weeks and it would be better if she didn't come around. He had refused to elaborate and had ended up hanging up on her. Her father had always had his quirks, but this secretiveness was new, and worried her.

"Well, when you see Mike, you tell him to stop in soon." Iris moved on to the next volunteer.

A cheer rose from the crowd by the roadside and Deni looked up to see the search and rescue crew, their bright blue parkas and yellow climbing helmets stand-ing out against the gray and white of snow and rock, climbing out of the canyon. The county's emergency management director, Sam Olsen, shook SAR Cap-tain Tony Meisner's hand as Tammy Patterson from the *Eagle Mountain Examiner* snapped a photo. "Great exercise," Sam said. A young man with a long blond ponytail, Sam was a familiar figure in town. He had visited Deni's eighth grade classroom earlier that year to talk about outdoor safety to kids for whom hiking, skiing and camping were as much a part of daily life as riding public transportation might be for city kids.

"Thanks, everyone, for all your help," Tony said, addressing the gathered volunteers. Several of the students, still sporting their "victim" makeup, stood with their parents, grinning broadly. Tanner Vincent, who had played the part of someone cut up by windshield glass, raised two thumbs up. "These kinds of exercises help us learn the best ways to respond to a real emergency," Tony continued. "Though let's hope none of what we pretended today ever becomes a reality."

Another cheer rose, though a shiver ran down Deni's spine. As much as no one ever wanted to deal with a tragedy like a school bus crash, the treacherous mountain passes and harsh winter weather around Eagle Mountain meant they were only one icy spot on the highway from a scenario very like what they had play-acted today.

She finished her coffee and stood to go. "Hey, Deni!"

Her heart beat faster as she turned to see Ryan striding toward her. He had removed his helmet, leaving his dark hair ruffled, and his cheeks were reddened by wind and cold. The effect was to make him look even heartier and more rugged. Or maybe she just thought that because she had been nursing a crush on him for weeks now. "It was good to see you today," he said, stopping in front of her.

She put up a hand to brush her hair back from her cheek and felt the stickiness of the fake blood. She must look horrible, with most of the makeup still in place that portrayed her as having hit her head. She guessed it was a good sign that that wasn't putting him off. "It's good to see you, too," she said.

"How did you end up volunteering for this?"

"When Sam came to recruit kids from my class, he asked if I'd like to participate, too." She shrugged. "It sounded like a fun way to spend a Saturday morning."

He chuckled. "If you say so."

"We can't all moonlight as superheroes," she teased, and felt the spark of heat from the look he gave her in response.

"Listen," he said. "I—"

But she didn't get to hear what he would have said next, as Sheriff Travis Walker interrupted with an announcement over the speakers in his SUV. "Everyone needs to leave the area immediately," he said. "Please return to your vehicles and leave now!"

"What's going on?" Ryan asked one of the deputies who was hurrying past.

"There's a suspicious object attached to the piling of the bridge." He pointed downhill, toward the highway bridge over Grizzly Creek, approximately one hundred yards from where Ryan and Deni stood.

"What kind of object?" Deni asked.

The deputy shook his head. "We don't know for sure, but it might be a bomb. We need to get everyone out of here, just to be safe."

A bomb. The word hit Deni like a punch in the gut. She swayed, suddenly dizzy. *No. This really can't be happening.*

Chapter Two

All the color had drained from Deni's face behind the garish makeup, and she looked as if she might faint. Alarmed, Ryan took her arm. "Hey, are you okay?" he asked.

"Just a little...shook up." She swallowed hard, and her eyes met his, terror making the pupils huge.

"Come on," he said. "Where's your car?"

"Back at the school," she said. "Another bus dropped us all off this morning." She looked around. "I think it was supposed to pick us up."

"I don't see it," Ryan said. "You can come with me."

She looked toward the bridge. The sheriff and three deputies stood on the edge of the road, looking down into the creek. "I should stay," she whispered, so softly he almost didn't hear her.

"We have to leave," Ryan said. He tugged her toward the parking area.

She didn't resist, but let him lead her toward his battered Tundra. He spotted Tony in the parking area, along with paramedic Hannah Richards. "How did they find this supposed bomb?" Ryan asked.

"Jake and Shane hiked down to the creek to make

sure no debris from the wrecked bus had washed into the water and saw it," Hannah said. She was dating Deputy Jake Gwynn, and Deputy Shane Ellis was his best friend.

"What did they see?" Deni asked. She didn't look as dazed as she had at first, though she was still pale, and her voice shook.

"Jake said it looked like a bundle of highway flares," Hannah said. "I don't know any more than that."

"Or it could be dynamite," Tony said.

"Lots of people knew we were doing this mock bus crash today," Ryan observed. "Maybe this is someone's idea of a joke."

"Sick joke," Tony said. He took his keys from his pocket. "Anyway, we'd better get out of here and let the cops do their job. Good work today." He nodded to Deni. "You, too."

Deni slid into the passenger seat of the Tundra and Ryan joined the caravan of vehicles headed back into Eagle Mountain. She remained silent until they were almost back to town, then she pulled out her cell phone. She punched in a number, then listened to the phone ring and ring. She stabbed the button to end the call and pocketed the phone again. "Everything okay?" Ryan asked.

"I was trying to call my dad," she said. "But he isn't answering."

"I doubt he could have heard about this already," Ryan replied. "I bet the sheriff didn't broadcast something like this on the scanner."

"I, um, I just promised to call him when the mock crash was over," she said.

"Your dad is Mike Traynor, right?" Ryan asked. "He lives in that off-grid cabin up Tennyson's Gulch?"

Her eyes flashed with something like alarm. "How did you know that?"

"I drove up there this fall to look at those cliffs for possible climbing," he said. "A buddy and I met your dad. He told us he thought the rock there was too brittle for climbing, and he was right. He introduced himself as Mike Traynor, so I figured, right age, same last name…"

She nodded. "That's him."

"Cool place he has, though I imagine it can be rough up there in winter. The county doesn't plow that road, does it?"

"Dad has a tractor and he keeps it clear," she said. "Or he uses his snowmobile. He says he likes the privacy."

"He's got that. Did you grow up there?"

She shook her head. "No. I grew up in Amarillo, Texas. Dad was a truck driver and my mother was a teacher."

"Like you."

"Yeah. Like me."

He wondered if he had said the wrong thing. She looked like she might be about to cry. He was really out of practice talking to women, or at least, talking to women he was attracted to. He searched for something else to say, to lighten the mood, but before he could think of anything, she said, "Mom died of cancer about a year and a half ago, about nine months after I moved to Eagle Mountain."

"I'm sorry," he said. "That must have been rough." His own parents were living happily in Albuquerque and though he didn't see them that often, he couldn't imagine not having them in his life.

"It was." She sighed. "Hard for me, but harder for Dad. I worried about him, in that big house by himself. When he said he had decided to move here, I was so happy."

She didn't sound happy now. "Why do I sense a *but* at the end of that sentence?" he asked.

"I thought he meant he'd get a condo in town, or a little house—not that he would move up into the mountains and live like...like some hermit."

He thought about what he could say to reassure her. She was still obviously upset, though he wasn't sure if she was worried about the supposed bomb, or her father or both. He probably shouldn't even get involved, but it tore at him, seeing her so distressed. "I can see how you would worry about him, living so remotely, and alone," he said. "But he seems like he's in good shape, and he's not that old, is he?"

She shook her head. "He's 55, and healthy. It's just..." She didn't finish the sentence, merely shook her head again.

They were almost to the school now. "My car is around back," she told him. "In the employee lot."

He slowed, but instead of turning into the lot, he said, "I don't like leaving you by yourself when you're still so upset. Do you want to go somewhere for a cup of coffee? Or something to eat?"

"I wouldn't be very good company right now," she observed.

"I'm not asking you to entertain me," he said. "I just want to make sure you're okay."

She straightened her shoulders, and looked him in the eye for the first time since she'd gotten into his car. "I'll be fine. I'm sorry I overreacted. The idea that we were so close to a bomb, with the children and everything…it was so unexpected."

"Of course it was." Her fear made more sense now—it showed how seriously she took her responsibilities toward her students. That made him like her even more. It made him want to take a risk and get to know her better. "Are you sure you don't want that coffee?"

She smiled, a genuine smile that warmed him deep inside. "Can I take a rain check? I have some things I have to do at home."

"You bet." He glanced in the rearview mirror and saw a car approaching, so he turned into the lot. "Maybe we can meet up one day after school."

"I'd like that."

He dropped her at her car, then drove to search and rescue headquarters. The metal building with three bays with roll-up garage doors was perched on the side of a mountain above town, convenient to both Caspar Canyon and Dixon Pass, as well as most of the trailheads leading into the high mountains, all locations of frequent callouts for the squad. Most of the other volunteers were already there, unpacking and inventorying gear, re-coiling ropes, restocking medical supplies and getting everything ready for the next emergency.

"How was it out there for you today?" Tony asked as Ryan passed him on the way to help with the climbing gear.

"Good." Ryan resisted the urge to rub the arm he had injured last month. Today's training exercise had been his first time to suit up as part of the team since the accident.

"No weakness in the arm?" Tony asked.

Ryan's first impulse was to lie and say he was fine—a hundred percent. But Tony and the other members of the team would depend on him in tough situations. If he wasn't up to the task, he needed to be truthful. "A little," he admitted. "But I'm getting a lot stronger."

Tony nodded. "You've come a long way. We'll keep you a light-duty until you're back full strength. Don't overdo it."

"I won't," Ryan said, though the temptation was always there. When Charlie Cutler, a convicted serial killer who was running from the law, had shoved him off the side of Mount Baker, he had been sure he would die. Thick snow had saved him from fatal injury, but after he had awakened from surgery to piece together his damaged arm, he had feared the life he loved, which revolved around climbing, and search and rescue, had ended. Hours of therapy and work were bringing him back, but he worried he would never be the person his fellow team members would trust to bear his share of the load.

It was bad enough knowing that if they knew about

his past, they probably wouldn't trust him ever again. He couldn't help thinking he had to work harder than other people to prove he was worthy of their faith in him. He pushed away these thoughts and moved to help the others. "Any more news on that bomb?" he asked as he helped rookie Austen Morrissey and Training Officer Sheri Stevens hang up coils of climbing rope.

"It was a real bomb, all right," Austen said. "The sheriff's department had to call in an explosives team from Junction to disarm the thing. I heard one of them say if it had detonated, it would have taken out the whole bridge and probably shut down the highway for months."

"Who would do something like that?" Sheri asked.

"A terrorist," Austen said.

"In Eagle Mountain?" Sheri shook her head. "Who cares what happens here?"

"They just finished that bridge last fall," Ryan added. "Didn't it win some kind of design award?"

"So maybe the designer's rival blew it up, jealous that he or she didn't win instead?" Sheri looked skeptical.

"More likely, it's just some crank trying to make trouble," Ryan speculated.

"The world is full of those," Austen said.

But Eagle Mountain wasn't, Ryan thought. Or at least, it hadn't been. Sure, bad things happened here—murders and robberies and natural disasters. But terrorism seemed pretty extreme for a small town in the middle of nowhere. And why try to take out a bridge that the bomber had to know would just be built again?

He didn't like to think about anyone trying to destroy the beauty and peace of this place. Eagle Mountain was his safe place. He had built a good life here after a bunch of big mistakes. He would rather focus on folks like Deni, who was so concerned about her students that even the prospect of danger to them upset her. She was the kind of person he wanted to be around.

The kind of person he wanted to know better.

AFTER TRYING UNSUCCESSFULLY to reach her father on his cell phone all Saturday, Deni got up early Sunday morning and decided to drive up to her father's place. Never mind that he had told her to stay away. She was his daughter and she had a right to see him. Not to mention, what if he wasn't answering her calls because he was sick or hurt? Who else but her would care enough to check on him?

Though Mike Traynor's cabin was only about ten miles from Deni's house in town, it took her almost forty-five minutes to reach the remote dwelling, the last half hour on a road that was little more than a narrow Jeep trail. She coaxed her Outback through snow-packed ruts that must have been made by her father's four-wheel drive truck, until she reached the gate where he usually parked in the winter. His truck, with its cab-over camper, wasn't there, and neither was the snowmobile he kept chained to a nearby aspen.

Ignoring the sick feeling in the pit of her stomach, Deni strapped on the snowshoes she'd brought with her, slipped on a pack and headed up the path through the bare aspens for the last half mile. The day was cold, but clear, and she hadn't gone very far before she stopped to peel off her parka. The sun beat down and ice crystals sparkled on every surface. If she hadn't been so worried, the effect would have been magical.

She followed the snowmobile's tracks, which told her her father had probably traveled this way to his parked truck. Had he loaded the snowmobile onto a trailer to pull behind the truck? Maybe he'd decided to go play on the snowmobile for the day. That was probably why he hadn't answered her calls—he was out of cell range.

If that was the case, she didn't need to be concerned. She began to feel a little better. That was probably it. As much as she worried about her father, he was a grown man, in good health. He had always liked being in nature and after a lifetime on the plains of Texas, he had fallen in love with these mountains just as Deni had.

Yes, he was grieving the loss of his wife, but maybe living in this remote location, surrounded by nature, was healing for him. Maybe he wasn't retreating from life so much as immersing himself in it. He had been excited when he first told her about the cabin. "There's nobody up there to bother me," he had said. She had argued that it wasn't good for him to be so alone but maybe that was what he had needed.

By the time she was in sight of the cabin, she had convinced herself she was worrying for nothing. The same way she had overreacted to news of that bomb at the bridge. Ever since her mother's death, her emotions had been so close to the surface, like exposed nerves sensitive to the slightest stimulus. No one told you that about grief—how it stripped you of so much, and just when you were sure you were getting better, something happened to rip off the scab and expose all your pain again.

Her father's cabin, built two decades ago as a summer retreat for a family from Houston, Texas, was a one-room structure with a sleeping loft and a deep front porch sided with slabs of rough cedar, protected from the elements by a rusting metal roof with deep eaves. Water came from a spring up above the structure, and an outhouse sat in a grove of aspen a hundred yards behind the house. Her father had added a three-sided shed where he kept his truck and the snowmobile, a workbench and an assortment of tools. The truck and snowmobile were gone from the shed, she noted. At the bottom of the porch steps she kicked off her snowshoes and mounted the steps to the porch. The door was in deep shadow, so she didn't see the big padlock until she was right on it. The lock was dull brass, as large as her fist with a hasp as big around as her finger. She had never seen it before. Then again, she had never been here when her father wasn't home.

She stared at the lock a long moment, then moved to the window beside the door and peered in. Dark drapes had been pulled over the window so she couldn't see inside. A shiver washed over her, and she hugged her arms across her chest as she paced the length of the porch. A neat stack of firewood sat at one end, a wooden bench her father had constructed of half logs at the other. Snow had blown in to dust the surface of the bench. It added to the abandoned atmosphere of the place, as if the person who lived here had left for good.

She was letting her imagination run away from her again. Resolutely, she pulled out her phone, intending to call her father again and let him know she had stopped by. Her father had installed a cell booster that allowed him to make and receive calls. She punched in her dad's number and was surprised when, this time, the call went straight to voice mail. A robotic voice recited her father's number—no name or instruction to leave a message and he would return her call. Her father had told her this was because he didn't want to hear from anyone, or return any calls, though he had agreed to make an exception for her.

"Dad, it's Deni. I drove up to the cabin to see you. I see the snowmobile isn't here, so I guess you're out riding it somewhere. Call me when you get back. Let's have dinner sometime. My...my Outback is making a funny noise and I'd like you to listen to it and tell me what you think."

That last was an afterthought, and a complete fabrication. Her Outback was running fine, but, while her father was as likely to turn down a dinner invitation as to accept it, he felt an obligation to keep her car running well and make minor repairs at her home. "There's no need to waste your money hiring someone who probably doesn't even know what he's doing," he would say. He had spent his lifetime repairing everything from cars to well pumps to small appliances. He didn't trust anyone else to do the job right.

She ended the call and started to tuck the phone into

her pocket once more when it vibrated in her hand. Startled, she checked the screen and saw an unfamiliar local number. "Hello?" she answered.

"Deni, it's Ryan. I called to see how you were doing this morning."

Butterflies rustled in her stomach. "Hi, Ryan. I'm good. How are you?"

"I'm good. Um… I wondered if you had time for lunch today?"

She checked the time—just a little after ten. "That would be nice."

"Want to meet at Mo's at noon? Or we could go someplace else, if you like."

"Mo's is fine." She had plenty of time to get back to her house and change.

"I guess you heard that was a real bomb they found," he said. "Though it was defective or something. The explosives team from Junction said it couldn't have detonated, the way it was wired."

The butterflies had all died, replaced by a sick heaviness. "Do they have any idea who put it there?" she asked.

"I don't think so. I'm sure they're looking. Hey, I've got another call coming in. Don't go away."

Before she could tell him goodbye, that she'd see him at noon, he was gone, leaving her on Hold. She couldn't hang up now, so she held the phone in one hand and put on her snowshoes, awkwardly fastening the clips with one hand.

"Sorry about that," Ryan came back on the line.

"And I'm sorry I'm going to have to cancel our lunch. That was Tony. Search and rescue got a callout."

"Oh no," she said. "What is it? I mean, are you allowed to say?"

"An injured climber in Caspar Canyon."

"I hope they're okay," she said.

"Me, too. I've got to go. Talk to you later."

"I'll look forward to that."

She ended the call and tucked the phone away, a little shaky with relief. Not that there was anything good about an injured climber, but at least it hadn't been another bomb.

She glanced toward the shed, and the workbench inside. She was tempted to go in there and look around—but what was she looking for? Her father had told her he had purchased dynamite to blast out a dam of ice that was blocking the spring. Why shouldn't she believe him? She had trusted her father her whole life.

It felt wrong not to trust him now. He had changed since her mother's death, but so had she. Loss changed people. Did she seriously believe her dad—her father—had been building bombs? Just because he had complained a lot lately about the cost of progress and development—just because he had said someone should "do something to slow all this down"—that didn't mean he had turned into a terrorist.

Chapter Three

Some search and rescue callouts were almost peaceful—long hikes in beautiful country to retrieve an injured hiker. A sense of urgency drove every action, but
the scene was controlled and orderly. Everyone had a
job to do and performed each task with choreographed
grace.

Then there were the calls like this one to Caspar
Canyon—a peaceful Sunday morning shattered by
chaos. Ryan and five other search and rescue volunteers drove into the canyon past police barricades, fire
trucks, ambulances and even a camera crew from a
Junction television station. Crowds of people milled
around outside an area cordoned off with yellow cau-
tion tape, and the air was thick with smoke.

Only it wasn't smoke, Ryan realized as they exited
the specially outfitted Jeep they had dubbed the Beast.
The air in the canyon was hazy with dust. Voices drifted
from the haze—shouts for help, screams of pain and
voices demanding order.

"Is that a helicopter?" fellow volunteer Eldon Ramsey
asked.

Ryan followed Eldon's gaze up toward the throbbing sound that was, indeed, a blue-and-white helicopter hovering over the canyon.

"Focus on the job, guys," Tony reminded them. He opened the back doors of the Beast and began unloading gear.

"What are we dealing with here?" Ryan asked as he helped maneuver a litter from atop the vehicle.

"The call said an injured climber in Caspar Canyon," Tony said. "No details."

"This is bigger than one climber who misjudged a move," Ryan said.

"The man you want is at the far end of the canyon." Sergeant Gage Walker with the Rayford County Sheriff's Department joined them. "There's at least one climber trapped under some fallen boulders," he said. "There are half a dozen other injured people, but EMS is seeing to them."

"What happened?" Tony asked. "Dispatch didn't provide any details."

Ryan had always thought of Gage as easygoing, a bit of a joker, even. Today, he looked grim. "We're not certain of all the details," he said. "But from what we've been able to determine so far, someone set off a bomb."

The words jolted through Ryan. He steadied himself with one hand on the side of the vehicle. "Was anyone killed?" he asked.

"Not yet," Gage said. "The ambulance transported Perry Dysert. I don't know any more than that."

Ryan knew Perry. The climbing community was a tight group and everyone knew everyone else. If that

murderer hadn't thrown Ryan off the side of a mountain a little over a month ago, he would have been here
this morning, too. A dozen questions half formed in
his head, but before he could ask them, Eldon clapped
a hand on his shoulder. "Come on," he said. "Let's take
care of this guy who's trapped."

The trapped guy turned out to be Garrett Stokes,
an experienced climber many of the younger rock rats
looked up to. His handsome, normally ruddy face was
pasty white and aged by pain as he lay half-buried in
a tumble of rock. "You're supposed to climb over the
boulders, not under them," Ryan said, as he dropped
his gear bag nearby. On closer inspection, Garrett's
lower body proved to be pinned by a jagged block of
black rock the size of a small SUV.

Garrett called Ryan a foul name, but with no malice
behind the words. RN Danny Irwin moved in to examine him, while the others studied the rock pinning
him. "We need a crane to lift that off," Eldon put in.

"The canyon is too narrow in this spot to bring in
anything bigger than a garden tractor," Tony said.

"Hydraulic jacks and a winch it is, then," Eldon
stated.

"If they make a jack big enough to lift that, I don't
think there's one in the county," Ted said.

"Maybe we could break the rock into pieces," Ryan
suggested.

"Not without risking further injury to Garrett," Tony
added.

Danny joined their huddle by the rock. "We're going
to run an IV to get some fluids and pain meds into

him," he said, keeping his voice low. "I'm worried about him going into shock. He's in a lot of pain, but there's no telling the extent of his injuries until he's out from under there. I expect there's broken bones, and maybe some internal injuries."

Ryan looked up at the waterfall of rock that had collapsed into the canyon. He thought this was the location of a route named McKenzie's Wall. It had featured a twenty foot slab of almost sheer, vertical rock that Ryan had never attempted. "Was he up there when the bomb exploded?" he asked.

"Looks like it," Eldon said.

"How is Garrett?" Sheriff Travis Walker, Gage's brother, joined them. He wore jeans and a black parka with a shearling collar, his badge clipped to his belt. Ryan wondered if he had been working at his ranch when the call had come in about the explosion. He didn't know the sheriff well, and preferred to steer clear of law enforcement, but Travis seemed like a good guy. If he knew about Ryan's past, he had never said anything.

"We need to get him out from under that rock," Danny said. "Sooner rather than later."

"We need to dig him out," Ted concluded.

The others turned to him. At sixty, Ted was the oldest member of Eagle Mountain Search and Rescue, a sometimes prickly personality who bristled at anything he took as an implication that he wasn't up to the job. But Ted was smart, and he had experience on his side. "We have to dig a trench and make room to slide him out from under the boulder," he said. "We'll have to be careful and dig it by hand, but if we can keep the rock from sinking lower as we dig, we should be able to free him."

"What tools do you need?" Travis asked.

Within ten minutes they had assembled an assortment of small shovels and one pickax, some lumber to shore up beneath the rock and several volunteers. They began excavating a trench around and beneath Garrett, who was mostly silent as they worked, numbed by the medication dripping into the line in his arm. Danny and paramedic Hannah Richards monitored the injured man as the others worked.

Ryan dug until sweat beaded on his forehead and his right arm, five-and-a-half-weeks postsurgery to insert a metal bar and seven screws, began to throb. "That's enough for you," Tony said, and relieved him of his shovel.

Reluctantly, Ryan stepped back to assume the role of spectator. "How much longer before they have him out?" a man standing next to Ryan asked. Compact and muscular, he wore a black jacket with an Explosives patch on the shoulder.

"Soon, we hope," Ryan said. "Any idea what happened?"

"The story we got was there was an explosion and the whole side of the canyon came down." The man eyed the debris critically. "My guess is the charge was set about halfway up, probably along a natural fault. It wouldn't take a huge charge to collapse one section of rock."

"Who would do something like that?" Ryan asked.

"Someone who doesn't like climbers. Or crowds in the canyon." The man met Ryan's gaze, a hardness there Ryan found unnerving. "Or maybe they did it just to prove they could."

"Stand back. We're going to try to move him now."

With one group of volunteers monitoring the rock for movement, and another prepared to shift Garrett an inch at a time, Danny gave the signal to begin. They shouted encouragement and directions to one another and two minutes later, Garrett was free. A cheer rose up from the crowd as Garrett was carried toward the waiting ambulance.

Ryan joined the others in collecting their gear. The explosives team took over the area, ordering everyone else away. "What do they expect to find in that mess?" Austen asked, looking over his shoulder at the men already sifting through the rock and gravel.

"They're hoping to find something to lead back to the bomber," Deputy Jake Gwynn said. He was also a trainee volunteer with search and rescue, and had been one of the group working to free Garrett.

"Do you think it's the same person who planted the bomb by the highway bridge?" Ryan wondered. Jake had shown him the photo he had taken of the sticks of dynamite wired to the bridge support. It had looked exactly like the bomb in cartoons, minus a ticking alarm clock.

"We don't know," Jake said. "We've been interviewing everyone we can find who was here this morning. We're hoping someone saw someone acting suspiciously at this end of the canyon, but there's a good chance the bomber planted the device late last night or early this morning, when no one else was around."

"It has to be the same person who planted that bomb by the highway bridge," Austen conjectured. "How many bombers could you have in one little county?"

"Even one is too many," Jake said. "We need to find him before someone else gets hurt."

Ryan and Austen made their way back to the Beast, arriving just as the ambulance with Garrett aboard pulled out. "Garrett is stable," Danny said before anyone could ask. "He was lucky the dirt where he fell was soft enough to allow him to sink in a little. He has a fractured ankle, torn ligaments in his right knee, some cracked ribs, a broken finger and bruised kidneys. Hopefully nothing worse, though they'll do scans and X-rays at the hospital."

Ryan flashed back to his own arrival at the hospital after being transported from a scree field by an army helicopter. Though his recall was fogged by all the painkillers he had been floating on, he had memories of many machines and people hovering over him.

"He was unlucky enough to have been up there on those rocks when a bomb exploded," Danny said. "But lucky enough to live to tell about it."

Someone had said the same about Ryan, though as he recuperated from his injuries, unable to compete in the annual ice-climbing festival and restricted from so many activities for weeks, he hadn't felt very lucky. He saw things differently now, and was grateful his fellow search and rescue members hadn't been tasked with retrieving his remains from that scree field.

"Ryan!"

He looked over his shoulder and was startled to see Deni pushing her way past a clot of spectators. "I just heard!" she said as she skidded to a stop in front of him, out of breath. "I saw the ambulance. Who was hurt?"

"Garrett Stokes," Ryan said. "Do you know him?"

"A little. Is he going to be okay?"

"We hope so," Ryan said. "He's pretty banged up. How much did you hear?"

"Someone said a bomb exploded and a bunch of people were hurt in Caspar Canyon." She looked past him toward the chaos in the canyon, and her fair skin blanched the color of aspen bark. "Is it true? Was it really a bomb?"

"The explosives guys are here from Junction," Ryan said. "So I guess so."

She swayed and he put a hand on her shoulder to steady her.

She leaned her weight against him. "Thanks," she whispered.

Everyone else was distracted by the work of reloading the Beast, so Ryan took Deni's arm and led her a little away from the others. "What's wrong?" he asked. "I know this kind of thing is upsetting, but what else is going on?" She hadn't struck him as the type to overreact, yet this—and the bomb they had found at the bridge yesterday—had her terrified to a level he couldn't account for.

"Oh, Ryan." She met his gaze, her eyes shiny with tears. "I'm so afraid."

He put his arm around her and held her close. She was trembling. "What are you so afraid of?" he asked.

"I think I know who the bomber is." She wet her lips. "Who it might be. I don't have proof, but…"

Her voice trailed away, and she stared at the ground. "Who?" he asked. "Who do you think did this? If you know, you have to tell."

"It's too awful." She shook her head and pushed away from him, but she didn't run away, as he half feared. Instead, she met his gaze full-on, her terror raw in her eyes. "I think… I think it might be my dad."

Chapter Four

As soon as the words were out of her mouth, Deni wanted to take them back. What would Ryan think? She was as good as accusing her father of being a terrorist. An attempted murderer. She put a hand to her mouth. "Please tell me no one died today," she said. She looked past him, into the canyon shrouded in a gray mist, bright yellow emergency tape snapping in the breeze that funneled through the area, hard-hatted emergency workers everywhere.

"No one has died yet, though some people have serious injuries," Ryan said. His voice was tight. She risked a glance and saw him watching her, concern tightening the vertical line between his eyebrows. "Why do you think your father did this?" he asked.

"He's been acting so strange lately. And he's said some things that didn't alarm me at the time, but when I think about them now…" She shrugged, helpless to explain her mixed-up feelings.

Ryan took a step back, his gaze fixed on her. "You need to tell the sheriff."

"I don't know anything," she said. "I only…suspect."

"Then tell him what you suspect. If you don't, you could end up in a lot of trouble yourself."

He was still staring at her. He didn't look angry, exactly. More afraid. "I haven't done anything wrong," she said.

He looked away, and she wondered if he would leave altogether, but after a moment in which he seemed to be struggling with something, his gaze met hers again, and a new calm showed in his eyes. "You could help a lot of people by telling the sheriff everything," he said. "Maybe especially, your father."

Would she be helping her dad by sharing her suspicions with the sheriff? Maybe she was wrong and her father really was off on a snowmobile trip and he had nothing to do with trying to kill people and destroy property. If she set law enforcement on him, he might never speak to her again.

But what if he was behind this? If he was really responsible for planting those two bombs, maybe he was past helping. The idea made her want to double over in pain.

She might not be able to help him, but she could prevent other people from being hurt and possibly dying. She had to try to save them, didn't she? "Would you come with me?" she asked. "To talk to the sheriff?"

Ryan blinked, and she was sure he was going to refuse. She started to apologize. After all, they scarcely knew each other. Why should he get involved in this mess with her dad?

"Come on." He took her arm and guided her past a

group unloading wooden barricades from the back of a truck. "I think I saw Travis over this way."

Ryan didn't ask what she knew, or why her father would do such a terrible thing. She was grateful for that. She didn't have any answers to give him. She only knew that as soon as she had heard about the bomb at the bridge, a lot of things began to make sense. A horrible sense, but it explained a lot about her father's behavior in the last year, and especially in the past few weeks.

Ryan kept hold of her arm and led her back toward the search and rescue crew. He was probably afraid if he let go, she'd run away. She was a little afraid of that too, and was grateful for his strong fingers anchoring her.

"I need to help Deni with something," he told the SAR commander, Tony Meisner. "I'll get a ride back to town with her."

Tony didn't even glance at her, his body halfway into the back of the vehicle. "Okay. Thanks for your hard work today."

They found the sheriff standing just inside the yellow plastic tape that cordoned off the blast site. Travis stood with his arms crossed, watching a group of men who wore dark jackets with EXPLOSIVES stenciled across the back. "Sheriff?" Ryan asked.

Travis turned, his gaze assessing them both. "What do you need?"

"Deni has some information," he said. "About the bomber."

Travis said nothing, merely looked at her, waiting.

"My father…" Her voice faltered, and she tried again.

"My father, Mike Traynor, has been acting oddly the past few weeks. He's said and done things… I thought it was just talk at the time. An unhappy man venting his frustrations. But now I'm worried he could have had something to do with this."

Still the sheriff said nothing. He looked at her steadily, as if weighing her words. "Could you come to the sheriff's department and give us a formal statement?" he asked after a long moment.

"Yes," she said. "Of course. And then what will happen?"

"We'll probably want to talk to your father."

"I don't know where he is," she said. "He isn't answering his phone, and I went up to his cabin this morning and he wasn't there. His truck and his snowmobile are gone and there's a padlock on the door."

Travis nodded. "We may need to search the place, but let's start with your statement." He turned to Ryan. "Could both of you meet me at the sheriff's department in fifteen minutes?"

"Yes, sir," Ryan said.

"You don't have to come if you don't want to," Deni said as they moved away, back toward the parking area. "I feel terrible about involving you in any of this." She had thought having him with her would make things easier, but now she felt guilty. And embarrassed. So much for thinking he would see her as someone he'd like to go out with. She would be lucky if he didn't avoid her the next time he saw her on the street. The missed opportunity to get to know him better might be one of the things she regretted most about this whole ugly situation.

"It's okay," he said. "And you heard the sheriff. He's expecting me to be there."

"Oh. Right." She fought back a wave of nausea at what she might be about to face. She didn't want to face it alone. "If you don't mind, it would be good to have a friend with me," she added.

He took her hand in his again, so warm and gentle. He looked a little less tense now. "Then I want to be there," he said.

Though she had passed the Rayford County Sheriff's Department countless times in her two years in Eagle Mountain, Deni had never been inside. The single-story brick building was unremarkable in its blandness, which she supposed was a benefit. No one greeted them when they stepped inside. "I guess we just wait here for Travis," Ryan said.

She sat in one of two straight-backed chairs by the door and studied the photographs on the wall of men and women in uniform, including a formal portrait of the sheriff, as handsome as a movie star, dark hair and dark eyes and sculpted cheekbones. His detractors liked to grouse that he had won election on looks alone, but most people she knew were fans of his no-nonsense approach to law enforcement, and the skilled group of deputies he had built to support him.

"I've never been in here before," Ryan said as he took the seat beside her.

"I guess that's a good thing," she mused. "I've never been here, either."

The front door opened and Travis walked in. "Come back with me," he said, and punched in a code that opened the door leading away from the reception area to a hall lined with offices. He led them to what she assumed was an interrogation room—gray walls, a single table with chairs and a camera situated overhead. "I want to record what you have to say," Travis said, as he flicked switches on another control panel inside the room.

Deni's stomach churned with nerves, but she took deep breaths and tried to remain calm. She sat in one of the chairs, Ryan next to her, and Travis recited the date and the name of everyone present, then settled opposite her. "Okay," he said. "Tell me everything you know that might relate to the bomb that detonated today at Caspar Canyon."

The first thing she knew was that whatever was going on had started long before today. "My father was a truck driver in Amarillo, Texas," she began. "It's what he did my whole life. He owned his own truck and contracted to various shippers. He said he liked being his own boss. He used to complain about regulations, and about bigger companies horning in and making it more difficult for independent operators like him to compete, but it was the same things his friends complained about, and I never felt like he meant anything by it."

She fell silent, not sure how to continue. Maybe the sheriff didn't want to know any of this. He probably wanted facts, but did she have any?

"When do you think that changed?" Travis asked.

She tried to pinpoint when her father had begun to

act differently. "My mother died of cancer 18 months ago," she said. "Of course Dad was devastated. They had been married 32 years. Not long after that, he decided to sell his truck and quit the business."

"Did that surprise you?" Travis asked.

"Yes, but he assured me he had been saving his money and that, with Mom's life insurance, he would be fine. When he told me he wanted to move to Eagle Mountain to be closer to me, I was thrilled."

"He has a place off-grid, right?" Travis clarified.

"Yes. In Tennyson's Gulch. That choice surprised me. I was hoping he would find a place here in town. Maybe even a part-time job, or at least some activity that would allow him to make friends. But he said all those years he spent on the road alone made him value solitude, and he really liked that cabin location."

"So your father had been acting a little differently for a while," Travis said. "Why do you think he might be connected to the bombs?"

He probably thought she was wasting his time, telling him the story of her life. She was trying to tell him about her father, but everything was so complicated. "Dad has never been the biggest fan of progress," she said. "But after he moved here, he complained a lot more about any changes. It was like, he thought he had found the perfect place to live and he didn't want anything to happen to change that. When they talked about putting in a traffic light at the highway intersection, he wrote letters to the editor of the paper and showed up at county commissioner's meetings to complain. So did other people—it's not like he was the only one."

Except with her dad, his protests had been different.
Angrier. "He said someone needed to stop people from
ruining the world," she said. "And…one time he told me
he thought the only way to get through to some people
was violence. That shocked me. I said, 'Dad, you don't
really mean that.' He looked right at me and said, 'Have
you ever known me to say anything I don't mean?'"

She shivered. Ryan put a hand on her back—just
resting it there lightly, the heat of his palm seeping
through her shirt. Comforting.

"Did Mike say anything specific about bombs or
explosions?" Travis asked.

"No. But he has a workbench up at his place and he's
always tinkering with things. He's very mechanically
minded. He can fix just about anything. And…and a
couple of weeks ago I was up there and I saw some dynamite on the workbench. It alarmed me, really. I asked
him about it and he told me not to worry—he was going
to use it to dynamite an ice dam that was choking off
the spring that provides his water."

"And you believed him?"

She felt miserable. "He's my father. He doesn't usually lie to me." But what if he had been lying this time?

Travis got up and retrieved a bottle of water from a
cooler in the corner and pushed it toward her. "Drink
some of this, then we'll go on."

She uncapped the bottle and drank, the cold of
the water shocking, making the muscles of her throat
clench. She replaced the cap but still held the bottle,
grateful for something to do with her hands. "Last
week, Dad called and said I wouldn't see him for a

few days. He had a new project he was involved in and he didn't want me coming around. He wouldn't give me any details, and he told me not to ask any more questions. He also told me—no, he ordered me—not to come up to his cabin for the next two weeks."

"Did he say anything else?"

"He told me not to worry and that I would understand everything soon enough."

"Why do you think your father is connected to the bomb at Caspar Canyon?" Travis asked. "Had he ever mentioned anything about that particular location?"

"When the ice-climbing festival was going on last month, he was so upset," she said. "He complained about the festival bringing all these tourists into town, about the climbers driving metal stakes into the rocks and stringing rope everywhere and not leaving nature alone. I tried to joke with him about it, but he was so upset. Really out of proportion, I thought at the time."

"Did he make any specific threats?"

"Not exactly. But he said if those climbers realized how dangerous their little hobby was, there wouldn't be so many of them. I didn't think anything of it at the time, but…"

Travis nodded. "Anything else you want to tell us?"

Deni sighed. She didn't want to tell him any of this, but she knew she had to. "The bomb at the highway bridge—the one that didn't go off. I wondered if he might have planted that one, too."

"Why is that?" Travis asked.

"He hated that bridge. I mentioned one day that I thought it was beautiful, and that it had won a design award, and he said expanding that new bridge had brought too many new people into town, that the next thing we knew they would be expanding the highway to four lanes and this beautiful little corner of paradise was being destroyed." She leaned across the table toward the sheriff, hoping she could make him understand. "That isn't like my father. It isn't the man I grew up with. Before, he always wanted to help people, not hurt them. He was the person everyone called to pull their car out of a ditch or fix a broken appliance. Something is really wrong with him for him to be so angry and…and mean."

"What did you find when you visited his cabin this morning?" Travis asked.

"His truck and his snowmobile were both gone, so I thought maybe he had decided to go riding—maybe camping, too. The truck has a camper on it. There was a padlock on the door—it looked new. I don't think he bothered to lock the cabin before. The drapes were pulled over the window so I couldn't see in. I've tried and tried to call his cell phone and he doesn't answer. The calls go straight to voice mail."

"What is your father's cell number?" Travis asked.

She recited the number and the sheriff made a note of it. "What about friends?" Travis asked. "Someone he might be with or have gone to visit?"

"He isn't close to anyone around here that I know of," she said. "He has coffee with Rouster Wilson pretty regularly, but mostly he kept to himself. He said he liked being alone."

"Is there anything else you think might be helpful?" he asked.

She shook her head. "I hope I'm wrong. I hope you find him and that he had nothing to do with any of this."

"You were right to come forward with your suspicions," he told her. "Thank you." He glanced at Ryan. "Do you have anything to add?"

"No, sir," Ryan said. "I'm just here to support Deni."

Travis stood, so they did also. "What are you going to do about my dad?" Deni asked.

"We'll try to get in touch with him," Travis responded. "We'll stop by his cabin. Try not to worry."

She almost laughed. Of all the useless advice people gave, "try not to worry" had to be at the top of the list.

They left the sheriff's office and returned to Ryan's truck. "Please take me home," she said. "Or to my car. I guess I need to get it."

"If you give me your keys, I'll get a friend to help me retrieve it," he said. "You look exhausted. Did you sleep at all last night?"

"Not really." She had been too worried about her father.

"Maybe you can get some rest this afternoon. Where do you live?"

She gave him directions to the small Victorian that had once probably served as a guest house or mother-in-law residence, but had been divided from the main house at some point and sold as a starter home. Deni thought it looked like a doll's house, painted pale gray and trimmed in dark blue, with a front porch just big enough for two chairs and a small table, and a single bedroom squeezed upstairs under the sloping roof, a half bath in what had once been a closet up there and a full bath downstairs in what might have been a back porch in the distant past.

"Thank you for bringing me home," she said when Ryan pulled into the driveway. "And thank you for staying with me. It was a little easier with you there."

"I'm not ready to leave you alone just yet," he said. "No offense, but you don't look well. When was the last time you ate?"

"I had coffee at breakfast." The thought of food made her stomach churn.

"That's what I thought." He switched off the truck engine. "It's late and I'm starving, so let me come in and make something for both of us."

She didn't have the strength to fight him, so she unlocked the door and let him inside. Her cat, a long-hair tortoiseshell named Cookie, yowled an angry complaint from her perch on the front windowsill, then jumped down and raced up the stairs. "That was Cookie," Deni said. "She's probably gone to hide under the bed. She doesn't approve of strangers."

"She'll learn I'm no one to be afraid of," he replied. "I like cats. And dogs. All animals, really. Better than a lot of people. Now, which way is the kitchen?"

"It's just through here." She started toward the back of the house, but he put a hand on her shoulder.

"You sit and rest," he said. "If you trust me to rummage in your cabinets, I'll find something for us to eat."

"I trust you." He already knew her worst secrets—what difference did it make if he discovered the sad state of her refrigerator or her love of cinnamon toaster pastries?

She sank onto the sofa, leaned her head back and closed her eyes, her interview with the sheriff replaying in her mind. She had no clue if Travis believed her or not. She only hoped they found her father, soon.

She might have dozed—the next thing she knew Ryan called her to the table. She roused herself, smoothed back her hair and shuffled into the kitchen. "I found some chicken noodle soup," he said, as he set a bowl on the table. "No crackers, so I made cheese toast."

She tried to remember how old that can of soup must have been. Maybe she had bought it last fall, when she had been fighting a cold. That wasn't too old, was it?

She sat and studied the food in front of her—a steaming bowl of soup with noodles floating in it, and two triangles of golden cheese toast on a saucer beside the bowl. She tasted the soup and her eyes widened. "This doesn't taste like any canned soup I ever had," she said.

"I found a bottle of sherry way back in the cabinet and added a little of that," he said. "And some fried onions."

She took another spoonful. "It's delicious. Is it a family recipe?"

He laughed. "My mother always said her favorite thing to make for dinner is reservations, and my father believes in paying other people to do things like prepare meals."

"So where did you learn to cook?" She sampled the

cheese toast. It was also perfect, the buttery cheese warm and velvety.

"I worked six months at a pretty high-end restaurant in Boulder," he said. "I was hired to wash dishes, but when the chef discovered I knew the difference between a shallot and a leek, he promoted me to sous chef."

"I'm impressed."

He shook his head. "Don't be. It just means I chopped a lot of vegetables and stirred a lot of pots. But I picked up a few useful ideas along the way."

"Tell me more about your family," she said. After all, he knew more than she wanted most people to know about hers.

"My mother and my father are both lawyers—corporate real estate law and contracts," he said. "My sister is also a lawyer, married to a lawyer. I'm the black sheep of the family."

At first, she thought he was kidding, then realized he wasn't. "Your parents aren't happy that you didn't choose law as a career?" she asked.

He looked away. "Let's just say they've accepted that's never going to happen."

Silence stretched between them, awkward and cold. She searched for something to get the conversation back on track. "You work for the Ride Brothers, don't you?" she asked.

He shifted, the chair creaking beneath him. "Yes. And I volunteer for search and rescue, serve on the Ice Festival planning committee, and when I'm not recovering from surgery, I climb. A lot. I'm happy."

He sounded more grim than content. He obviously wasn't the type to volunteer much about himself, but she wanted to keep him talking.

"I heard about your accident," she said. "When that escaped killer pushed you off Mount Baker. You were hurt pretty bad, weren't you?"

He made a face. "I had to have a couple of surgeries but I'm almost as good as new. Another few weeks and I'll be able to climb again."

He reached over and collected her empty bowl. "I'll do the dishes."

"No!" she protested. "You've already done so much."

"I insist."

In the end, they did the dishes together. When everything was washed and dried and put away, she realized she had drawn out their time together as long as possible. "I'd better let you go now," she said. "Thanks for staying. And for the soup."

"It was your soup," he countered.

"But you made it special."

His gaze met hers, searching. "Are you sure you'll be all right?"

"I'm sure." It was a lie, but one she needed to tell him, and herself. "Goodbye."

She walked him to the door, where he pulled on his coat, then bent to kiss her cheek.

Except she turned her head, and caught his lips; what had been intended as a brief caress transformed into more—a delicious meeting of their mouths that proved cooking was not his only talent.

He pulled back first, cheeks flushed, looking a little

stunned. "Um, I'd better go," he said, and before she could object, he turned and left.

She moved to the window and watched him go. He was definitely an intriguing guy. He spent much of his spare time helping others, many of them people he didn't even know. He was good-looking and friendly, but he also held himself a little apart. This reserve had surprised her, but it also made her want to find a way to break past it. Not because she didn't respect his privacy, but because she thought Ryan Welch was a man worth knowing better.

Chapter Five

Going home with Deni had been a bad idea. Ryan knew it, yet he had done it anyway, which proved he hadn't learned all that much in the past six years.

That wasn't right. He had learned how easily he could be led astray. Especially when his normal instincts to want to help someone in trouble overruled his common sense. Yes, Deni was a really nice woman, at least on the surface. And yes, he was attracted to her. But when he learned her father might be some kind of domestic terrorist, he should have run away and never looked back.

The entire time they were sitting in the sheriff's department, he had been waiting for Travis to ask him how he was involved in all this. Had he known about the dynamite and bombs? He was a climber—had he helped plant that bomb in Caspar Canyon? Because guilt by association was a real thing, wasn't it?

And by that time, Travis could have said, "We know about your prison record. So it wouldn't surprise us at all if you were in trouble again."

He stood in the shower, the hot water cascading over

him, and tried to wash away the old fear and anger. This was the kind of thing he appreciated now—the ability to take a shower as long as he wanted. Alone. With the water as hot as he wanted. He hadn't been able to do that in prison.

He shut off the water and slicked back his hair, then reached for a towel and blotted water from his eyes. Two years and twenty-nine days he had spent in a Colorado prison, all because he had fallen for the wrong woman. Tracy had known just what to say to persuade him to help her. He had known what he was doing was wrong, but had done it anyway. Because she needed him.

Because he thought he was in love.

He finished drying off and pulled on jeans and a T-shirt. His injured arm ached worse than usual, so he swallowed some ibuprofen, then lay on his bed and stared at the ceiling.

It wasn't fair. Not big news, but he had to acknowledge his resentment over this fact, all the same. For the first time since getting out of prison three years before, he had decided to risk asking someone out. If he let Deni get to know him, maybe she wouldn't hold his record against him.

But the last thing he needed was any association, however tangential, to criminal activity. Especially something like these bombs.

He closed his eyes, and saw Deni's face again—hurt, confused, trusting him to help her. He remembered the feel of her lips on his, the taste of her. He had wanted her so badly in that moment. He still felt the ache.

He ought to be used to that by now. His life these days was as much about what he couldn't have as what he could. He had told himself walking around free with a job he enjoyed and volunteer work that mattered was enough.

But then he had met Deni, and he realized he had been lying to himself all along.

DENI DIDN'T HEAR from anyone for the next two days—not her father, or the sheriff. Not even from Ryan. The barista at the coffee shop said he had told her he was going out of town for a couple of days, so that was probably the reason for his silence.

She tried to put her worries about her father out of her mind. She told herself not to obsess over things she couldn't control. But she continued to call her father's number several times a day, leaving messages that all sounded the same: "Dad, I'm worried. Please call me," until a recorded voice informed her that "The recipient's voice mailbox is full. Please try again later."

At school, she put on her usual pleasant expression for her students. Eighth grade was a tough year for so many of them—they were too old to be little kids, and too young to be grown. Hormones, awkward growth spurts, shifting friendships, desperate crushes and academic challenges made for plenty of crises for Deni to address and wounds to soothe. With her own emotions so raw, she sympathized even more with her students.

Tuesday evening, she was on her way home from a yoga class when she saw Ryan headed into Mo's Pub. She thought about stopping and going in after him.

She could pretend to be surprised to see him. Maybe they would end up having dinner together. Instead, she drove on. She liked Ryan a lot—liked him too much to drag him into her current drama. He might argue that he was already well into it, having sat through her interview with the sheriff—not anyone's idea of a good first date. He already knew how bad her father might be and that hadn't put him off.

But she had a feeling things might get worse before they got better. Her father was bound to turn up soon, and even if he had nothing to do with those bombs, questions would be raised. Relationships were difficult enough to launch without adding in family problems.

Wednesday morning, she still hadn't thought of a good way to explain to Ryan that she needed to pull back, so she skipped stopping for coffee. She was being a coward, not to mention really rude, blowing off a nice guy this way. She would talk to him and explain everything—soon. She just couldn't deal with it right this minute.

For one thing, she had come up with a plan to try to track down her dad. Wednesday evening, the town council was meeting to discuss a variance request by the people who had converted a historic building downtown into a hotel. Though the Nugget Hotel had been open less than a year, the owners were proposing to triple its size. The council had indicated that they were in favor of the proposal, but loud protests from a number of locals, including her father, had led them to schedule one more public forum to discuss the issue. After tonight's public comment session, the council would cast its vote.

Deni had little interest in the issue, but she remembered how upset her father had been about the proposed expansion, and how he had rejoiced over the delay in the vote. He wouldn't miss the opportunity to have one more say about the matter. If he was anywhere nearby, Deni felt sure he would show up for the meeting.

Seven o'clock found her in the crowded meeting room upstairs at the county courthouse. She took one of the last vacant seats and scanned the crowd. People filled the ranks of folding chairs and stood along the wall. She saw plenty of familiar faces—the school principal nodded to her and several parents waved. But her father was nowhere in sight.

Council chair Mac Rodriguez stood and banged a wooden gavel. A slight man with a hawk nose and thick silver hair, Mac had a sonorous voice that surprised Deni every time she heard it. "I call this meeting of the Eagle Mountain Town Council to order," he intoned. The four council members flanked him behind the long table on the dais. They stared out at the crowded room with the expressions of guests at a shotgun wedding—everyone agreed this meeting had to happen, but no one really wanted to be there.

People continued to arrive as the first items on the agenda were checked off—approval of the minutes from the last meeting, a report from the town planner on the purchase of a new riding lawn mower and recognition of a high school student who won a national essay-writing contest. The door at the back of the room creaked loudly when anyone opened it, and every time, Deni turned around to see who had entered.

The third time she turned, a man with a bushy white moustache, a white Stetson pulled low over his eyes, stepped in. He wore starched Wrangler jeans and a blue-and-white-striped Western shirt and no jacket, despite temperatures in the twenties. Her dad was like that. "I'm not going to put on a coat to walk from my truck to the restaurant," he would say. She tried to get a better look at the man, but he had already been swallowed up by a new group entering the room. Something about him was familiar. Was he a friend of her father? Should she ask him if he had seen her dad recently?

"Now we will open the floor for public comment on the variance request from Nugget Hotel," Mac said. "Speakers who have signed in will have no more than five minutes to state their case. When your name is called, please come up to the microphone at the front of the room." He glanced at the clipboard on the table before him. "Glenda Nassib, you're first."

While Glenda, a tall, angular woman with close-cropped white hair, made her way from the back of the room, Deni tried to figure out where she knew the guy with the moustache.

"I know that growth is important to any economy," Glenda said. "But there is a right way and a wrong way to handle that growth, and I don't think allowing the Nugget to add two more floors and a new annex that will take up half a block downtown is the way to go. It's going to look as out of place in Eagle Mountain as a dress shirt on a sheep."

The shirt! Deni sat upright. That blue-and-white Western shirt was identical to one she had given her dad for Father's Day last year. Or his birthday. She jumped up. Mac banged his gavel. "Ma'am, do you wish to be recognized?"

"Oh! No, I, um, no." She sat back down to mild laughter from those around her, and wished someone would trip the fire alarm, or provide some other distraction. She waited until Glenda started speaking again before she turned to look back to where the man with the white moustache had been standing, but all she could see was the top of his Stetson.

The door at the back of the room opened, squeaking loudly, and Deni turned again to see the hat—and the broad shoulders covered in the blue-and-white cotton—disappearing into the hall. She would have recognized that back anywhere, having followed it so many places over the years.

She jumped up and, mumbling apologies, pushed her way down the row to the aisle. Once clear of other people's feet and knees, she hurried to the door, hoping everyone would assume she had remembered something she had to do, and no one would feel compelled to come after her.

She burst into the hall in time to see the man she was after disappearing through the exit door at the far end. "Dad!" she shouted. "Wait!"

She ran, the hard soles of her boots echoing on the polished wood floor. She was almost to the exit when she collided, hard, with a man in a black leather duster.

"Deni! Are you all right?" Ryan gripped her shoulders firmly.

She looked past him, to the now closed door. "I thought I saw my dad," she said. "In the council meeting. I was trying to catch him."

Ryan followed her gaze to the door, then took her hand and pulled her forward. "Come on. If we hurry, maybe we can catch up with him."

They ran onto the sidewalk and scanned the cars parked along the curb, then hurried to do the same on both sides of the courthouse. "He's not here," Deni said, disappointment heavy in her stomach.

"You're sure it was your father?" Ryan asked. "I came in just now and the only person I saw was some cowboy in a white hat with a Sam Elliott moustache."

"That was him," she said. "Or at least, I'm pretty sure that was him."

"I didn't know your dad had a moustache."

"He doesn't. And he doesn't wear a Stetson. I think he was trying to disguise himself. But he was wearing the shirt I gave him for Father's Day last year. And when he left the room, I recognized his back. It was him." She pulled out her phone and hit the speed dial for her father's number. It rang and rang, then disconnected. "What am I going to do now?" she moaned.

"Let's get some coffee and talk about it," he said.

Now that she wasn't so focused on following her father, she realized how close they were standing. She caught the scent of mint on his breath, and cold leather from his jacket, and remembered his hands gripping her shoulders, steadying her. "I don't want to keep you from the meeting," she said—though really, that was exactly what she wanted, now that he was here.

"I didn't come in here for the meeting," he said. "I came in to pay my water bill." He nodded toward a slot for depositing payment after hours. "Then I saw you and thought maybe something was wrong."

My father might be planting bombs around town. Isn't that wrong enough? But she didn't say it. Instead, she zipped up her parka. "Coffee sounds good."

THE ONLY PLACE to buy coffee after seven at night was the ice cream shop next to the post office, where the bored teenager behind the counter had to be persuaded to brew a fresh pot. "No one ever orders coffee this late," he said. "Or almost never."

"We want coffee," Ryan insisted. He put a dollar in the tip cup.

"Suit yourself," the student said, and turned to dump beans in the grinder.

Ryan returned to the table where Deni waited. Hair windblown and cheeks flushed from the cold, she made a particularly attractive picture—except for the pinched look around her eyes and the dark circles that told of sleepless nights. He had been forcing himself not to contact her, but he hadn't been able to turn away after she had literally run into him. "I guess your dad is one of the people who is against the hotel expansion," he said. "So you thought he'd be at the council meeting?"

"Yes. And he was there. When he saw me, he left. Why is he avoiding me?"

"Maybe he doesn't want to get you into trouble,"

Ryan supplied. "If he is involved somehow in these bombs, he could be trying to protect you."

"I don't want to be protected," she said. "I want him to stop trying to kill people."

The teenager working there dropped a spoon or something, and Deni flushed a deeper pink and lowered her voice. "If I could talk to him, maybe I could find out where he's been, and if he had anything to do with those bombs."

"I know he's your dad, but maybe you should leave finding him to the cops," Ryan said. "I mean, if he is involved with this, maybe it's because he's had some kind of mental breakdown or something."

"It has to be something like that," she observed. "My dad wouldn't hurt anyone."

"Coffee's ready!" the teenager called, and Ryan went to get it. He set one cup, along with two creamers and two sugars, in front of Deni.

A smile broke through some of her worry. "You remembered how I like my coffee," she said.

"I've been paying attention." He added a packet of sugar to his own cup. "I've been trying to work up the nerve to ask you out for a while."

The smile faded a little. "And I turn out to have a father who could be on the sheriff's department's Most Wanted list."

"Yeah, well, not ideal." Way to state the obvious, he thought.

"I really like you," she said. "But my life is such a mess right now." She met his gaze. "I could use a friend, even though you're not exactly seeing me at my best."

What he saw was a beautiful, hurting woman who was as alone in the world as he was. The look she gave him then made him feel ten feet tall and unbreakable. "I could be your friend," he said, even while part of his brain was screaming *No!*

"Thanks." She lifted her cup to her lips. "I heard you were out of town for a couple of days," she noted after she drank. Was she changing the subject because she sensed his uneasiness? Or maybe she just wanted to focus on something besides her own troubles.

"I went to see Garrett Stokes," he said. "He was transferred to Anschutz Medical Campus."

"He was one of the climbers hurt in the bombing, wasn't he?" she asked. "How is he doing?"

Some of the lightness left Ryan as he remembered his visit with his friend. "He's probably going to lose his leg above the knee," he said. "There's too much damage to repair."

She pressed her hand over her mouth, her eyes wide and glistening. "I'm so sorry," she whispered.

"Hey, it's not your fault. And Garrett is going to be okay. He's already talking about getting a special prosthesis for climbing. I heard Perry is doing good, too. Word is he'll get to come home in just a few more days."

She nodded. "I heard that, too. But I haven't heard anything from the sheriff—or from my dad."

"Maybe Mike has a new girlfriend and he's afraid you won't approve. Or...a boyfriend?"

That surprised a laugh from her. "Either way—I might be surprised, but I wouldn't disapprove," she said. "I want Dad to be happy. It would be a relief to know he had found someone. And he should know that. We've always been close."

He envied her that. His dad was not an especially warm person and from a young age Ryan had been aware that he was not the son his father would have wanted. But there was no sense dwelling on that.

"I was thinking about going back up to my dad's place on Sunday," she said.

"Maybe you should leave that to the sheriff," he said.

"I called today and it sounded like they haven't done anything," she said. "I can't sit here and do nothing. If I can get inside his cabin, maybe I'll find something to tell me where he is."

"There's been a lot of snow up there," Ryan said. "You shouldn't go by yourself."

"I'll be okay." She sipped her coffee. "But if you don't hear from me, you might check to make sure I'm not stuck in a snowdrift."

She said the words as if she was kidding, but he had been on enough search and rescue calls to know traveling those mountain roads in winter was a real risk. "I have to teach an avalanche class on Saturday, but I could go with you Sunday," he said. "That is, if you haven't heard from him by then."

"You don't have to do that," she said.

"I'll worry about you if I don't." If she got hurt up there by herself, he would feel responsible.

"Do you have a key so we can get inside?" he asked.

"No. There's a big new padlock on the door."

"Is there another way in? A window, maybe?"

"Maybe. At least we could try." She smiled—just a brief upturn of her lips and warming of her eyes. Enough to make him feel good again. "Thanks. At least I'd be doing something, instead of calling his phone repeatedly and worrying."

"Garrett told me he never saw the bomb—no one did," Ryan said. "It must have been planted way down in the rock. And the explosives expert I talked to at Caspar Canyon that day said whoever did it knew just where to put the bomb to bring down that wall. That sounds to me like an expert—not a man who worked all his life as a truck driver."

"You're right," Deni said. "But that doesn't mean Dad couldn't have studied the matter and learned. He has a knack for figuring out engines and things like that."

"Explosives aren't like a car," Ryan explained. "And the sheriff's office hasn't questioned you anymore. I think that means your dad isn't their top suspect."

"I guess I hadn't thought of it that way." She met his gaze again. "Do you think our parents worried about us this much, when we were growing up?"

"I know I gave mine plenty to worry about," he said. "I still do, I imagine."

"I'm beginning to think I didn't worry mine enough," she added. "Maybe he wouldn't be doing this to me now."

"You've got me on the case now," he said. "Between the two of us, we'll track him down." Every word was pure bravado. He didn't know the first thing about finding a man who wanted to stay missing. But he wanted Deni to feel better, and seeing the way her expression lightened a little at this comment, he determined to do everything in his power to locate Mike Traynor—and then give him a lecture on how lucky he was to have a daughter like Deni in his life. Ryan hadn't known her that long, but he was smart enough to have already figured out that she was special.

Chapter Six

Ryan had volunteered to teach this avalanche safety course with search and rescue commander Tony Meisner shortly before the accident that put him in the hospital. He had insisted on keeping the commitment even in the early days, when his prognosis was less clear. "If there's anything too physical for me to handle—though there won't be—you can do it," he had told Tony. "All I have to do is talk, and there's nothing keeping me from that."

Now that the day of the course had arrived, Ryan felt stronger than ever, though his doctor had cautioned he wouldn't be at full strength for a few more months yet. No worries about that today. This was a beginner's course, focused on the correct use of an avalanche beacon, techniques for reading snow conditions and avoiding a slide, and what to do if you or a companion was caught in an avalanche.

The class convened at the parking area in Galloway Basin, a popular backcountry ski area. The lot was almost full of cars by the time Ryan and Tony pulled in. They exchanged greetings with several skiers who were heading out, then went in search of their students. Today's class consisted of six people: two couples, a single man and Deputy Jake Gwynn, a new search and rescue trainee who was here to fulfill part of his training requirements.

Jake met them at the back of Tony's SUV and helped unload the gear while the others huddled at the edge of the lot, talking amongst themselves. "Any news about that bomb that went off in Caspar Canyon?" Tony asked the question that was tops in Ryan's mind.

"We haven't found the bomber," Jake said.

"Is it the same guy who planted that bomb at the highway bridge?" Tony asked.

"Maybe."

Jake clearly didn't want to discuss this, but Tony pressed. "Well, is it or isn't? What's the big secret?"

"The materials used in both bombs were the same, as far as we can tell," Jake said. "That's all I can say."

"So, any suspects?" Tony asked.

Jake glanced at Ryan, who figured he had probably read the transcript of the interview with Deni. "We've got a couple of people we're looking at, but nothing very solid."

A couple of people. So Mike Traynor wasn't the only possible bomber on their radar. Deni would be relieved to hear that.

The three of them quickly transformed a corner of the parking lot into an outdoor classroom. Everyone introduced themselves and Ryan launched into the first lecture, using a whiteboard on an easel to illustrate points as necessary. They had a discussion about different types of terrain and snow condition, using their surroundings as examples.

Then it was Tony's turn. He set up a device like the ones used in some ski resort backcountry gateways and a few popular remote rural areas and showed everyone how to test their beacons using the device. Then everyone paired off to practice using their beacons in send and receive mode.

After a break, they moved out onto the slopes for instruction on testing the quality of the snow, hazards to look for, best practices when skiing in an area with heightened avalanche danger and who to contact for information on that day's conditions. "You're skiing for free in some amazing terrain," Tony said. "But it's up to you to do your homework and be prepared for the worst. If something happens, search and rescue will respond and try to save you, but the truth is, most avalanche rescues are body retrievals by the time we arrive."

Ryan watched the faces of everyone present as this information sank in. No one set out on a beautiful winter morning thinking about the possibility that they could die that day, but part of this training was to have them do so, and to take all the precautions they could to prevent that from happening. "Backcountry skiing is risky," he said. "But there are ways to mitigate the risks. Taking this course today is one of them. Implementing what we teach you—every time you set out— is another."

The rest of the day was spent practicing what they had learned—taking samples of the snow, probing terrain, reading a slope and avoiding the most unstable conditions and finally, using the beacons to locate one another—on top of the snow. They shared tips on what to do if caught in an avalanche that might provide that little extra cushion that would allow you to survive until your friends could find you and dig you out. Though Tony and Ryan had both had the unpleasant task of digging out the bodies of people who had died in avalanches, they had rescued survivors, too. It wasn't impossible to come out alive, and even uninjured, but it did require good equipment, good technique and a lot of luck.

By two in the afternoon they were packing up to leave. Jake helped haul their gear back to Tony's SUV. When everything was loaded in, Ryan pulled him aside. "I know there are probably things you aren't supposed to tell me," he said. "I just want to know if you've had any luck locating Mike Traynor? Deni is really worried about him."

"I'm sorry. We haven't heard anything from him. We put out a bulletin saying we wanted to talk to him in connection with a case, with his description and information about his truck, but nothing has come up. Sergeant Walker went up to his cabin, but didn't find anything outside, and we don't have a warrant to go inside. He's not answering his phone, either."

"He won't return Deni's calls, which she says is unusual."

"It's possible he went somewhere on that snowmobile and had an accident," Jake said. "Depending on where he was and how badly he was hurt, he might not be found until spring."

Jake meant Mike's body might not be found until spring—or ever. People went missing in these mountains every year. Some of them were never found. "Deni thinks she saw her dad at the town council meeting Wednesday evening," Ryan said. "He was one of the people who spoke out against the hotel expansion before. She attended the meeting, thinking he might show up."

"No one else said anything about this," Jake said. "I wasn't at the meeting, but Deputy Douglas and her husband, Nate, were there. They would have been watching for him, too."

"Deni says Mike was wearing a disguise—a big white moustache and a Stetson pulled down low over his eyes. She didn't recognize him at first, but he was wearing a shirt like the one she had given her father as a gift."

Jake looked doubtful. "Lots of people probably have the same shirt."

"Deni was sure this was her dad."

"Did she speak to him?"

"No. When he saw her, he left in a hurry. She went after him—we both did. But he was gone."

"Do you think this man was Mike Traynor?" Jake asked.

"I never saw him. And I only ever spoke to Mike once, so I'm not sure I'd recognize him if he looked at all different. But Deni was sure it was him, and it does seem odd that someone would come to the meeting and leave before the first speaker had finished."

"You can tell Deni we're still looking for her father," Jake said. "And if she sees him again, call us right away."

"She was talking about going up to his cabin tomorrow and trying to get inside," Ryan said.

Jake frowned. "I can't stop her from doing that, but tell her to be careful. If she finds anything suspicious, don't touch it. Leave and call us to come take a look. If Mike is involved in this somehow, she doesn't want to compromise any evidence."

"I'll tell her," Ryan said. He didn't want the sheriff's office to know he had agreed to go with Deni.

"Tell her we haven't found anything linking her father to the bombs," Jake said. "We're still looking, but right now we're focused on a man who used to work for the highway department. Apparently he had a lot of experience with explosives and was upset because he had been fired for using some state equipment to do some work at his house without permission."

"She'll be relieved to hear that. Thanks."

"You didn't get it from me," Jake said.

"Understood."

Ryan told himself he should wait until tomorrow to talk to Deni, but instead of heading to his apartment over the art gallery, he drove to her house. Maybe hearing Jake's update on the search for her father would change her mind about going up to his cabin. She answered the door wearing pink leggings and an oversize sweatshirt, a pink bandana tied over her hair. "I was cleaning house," she said, and looked down at the rag in her hand.

"I have some news," he told her. "Not much, but it might cheer you up."

"Come in." She held the door open wider. A vacuum cleaner stood in the entry, and the furniture was pulled out from the walls. He caught a glimpse of the cat on the stairs before it vanished into another room. Deni tossed the rag onto the coffee table and sank onto the sofa. "So, what's the news?"

He sat beside her. "Deputy Jake Gwynn was one of the students in the avalanche safety class I taught this morning," he said. "I asked him if they had been able to locate your father. He said no, but that they hadn't found anything connecting Mike to the bombs. In fact, they have another suspect—a disgruntled highway department employee who is supposedly experienced with explosives."

Her lip trembled, and she leaned back against the cushions. "Really?"

"That's what he said. He also told me not to pass it on to anyone else. I'm sure they don't want the information getting back to their suspect. But he said it was okay to tell you. They're still looking for your father, but they don't think he had anything to do with those bombs." Those weren't Jake's exact words, but they were what Ryan had taken away from their conversation.

Deni grabbed his hand. "Thanks for telling me. It's a huge relief—though I'm still worried about Dad."

"Maybe the sheriff will find him soon."

"I've been thinking, and I'm pretty sure we can get in the back window at Dad's cabin," she said. "If I have to, I'll break a windowpane and undo the lock. Dad can argue about it with me later."

"So you're still determined to go up there."

"Yes. I'm feeling more positive about checking out the place now that you've agreed to go with me."

Here was his chance to back out. He could make up some excuse about having forgotten another commitment. But he couldn't do it.

He stood. "I'll let you get back to your cleaning. See you at nine in the morning?"

She stood and walked with him to the door. "Thank you for talking to Jake about my dad. You can't imagine how much better I feel."

She looked up at him, eyes shining. He wanted to kiss her—his gaze flickered to her lips. But the last thing he needed was to get any more involved with her. His mind knew that, even if his body didn't agree.

Then she slid her hand around the back of his neck and pulled his head down to her. There wasn't any hesitation in her kiss, and there was more passion behind the gesture than he would have expected for a simple thank-you. He wrapped his arms around her and pulled her against him, enjoying the feel of her body close to his. She was soft and warm and smelled like flowers and vanilla. Irresistible.

She pulled away, still smiling. "See you tomorrow," she said.

If she had intended for him to spend the next fifteen

hours thinking about her, that kiss had guaranteed she would figure prominently in his dream. So much for keeping his distance.

DENI WOKE FEELING better than she had in a week, but her good mood scarcely lasted past her first cup of coffee. The sheriff's department didn't think her father was the man who had planted those bombs, so neither should she. But if he wasn't hiding because he had done something wrong, where was he?

Had he gone somewhere on his snowmobile and been injured? But if that was the case, he wouldn't have been at the council meeting Wednesday, and she was positive the man she had seen had been him. He had been wearing a disguise and hadn't wanted her to see him. Why? Nothing about this situation made sense.

By the time Ryan arrived with a bag of muffins from the bakery, she had worked her stomach into knots again. He said hello, then studied her, picking up on her agitation. "Are you having second thoughts about going to your dad's place?" he asked.

She shook her head. "I've just been thinking about seeing Dad at the courthouse Wednesday. Why was he avoiding me?"

"Maybe he doesn't want to involve you in whatever he's doing," Ryan said. "That could be a good thing."

"Whatever he's up to, I need to know," she said. "I'm strong enough to deal with the truth." Though she didn't feel very strong right now.

Ryan offered to drive, and his truck seemed better equipped for heavy snow than her Subaru. The snow

on the forest service road leading into Tennyson Gulch
had thinned, exposing gravel in places. Ryan's Tundra
bounced over the ruts and through soft spots with ease.
Sun shone down through dark green ponderosa pines
and burnished the bare white trunks of aspen. "It's been
a long time since I've been up here," Ryan said. "How
did your dad ever find this place?"

"It was listed with a local real estate agent," she
said. "I think the family who owned it used it as a
summer getaway and had had it for years and years. I
was shocked when he told me he planned to live here
year-round. I thought he spent so many years in Texas
because he hated snow. But he told me he enjoyed the
challenge, and for a while it seemed to make him happy,
fixing up the place." She had been glad to see him focus
on something positive, emerging from the grief that had
engulfed him after her mother's death.

"The turnoff is just up here." She pointed to the
right. "There's a parking area. We'll have to snowshoe
in from there."

They parked and she got out of the truck and studied the tire tracks in the flat, cleared off area beside
the trail that led to her father's cabin. "What are you
looking for?" Ryan asked.

"I don't know." Did she really think she could recognize her father's tire treads in all these tracks? "I guess
these tracks are from the sheriff's deputies," she said.
"They weren't here when I stopped by the other day."

They strapped on snowshoes and headed down the
path through the trees to the cabin. When they emerged
into the clearing in front of the structure, she paused to

look around. "Nothing looks any different than when I was here last Sunday," she said.

"What's over there?" Ryan asked. He nodded toward the open shed to the left of the cabin.

"Dad parks his truck and snowmobile in there," she replied. "And there's a workbench and some tools and stuff."

"Let's have a look." He led the way to the shed, which was mostly empty, save for a couple of gas cans, some gardening tools and a chainsaw. Ryan examined the hand tools scattered across the workbench. "Nothing suspicious here," he said. "Did you say your dad had some dynamite?"

"It was in a box on the workbench when I stopped by to see him a couple of weeks ago," she said. "It's not here now. He said he was going to use it to get rid of an ice dam that was blocking his spring."

He nodded. "Are you ready to try the house?"

"I am—and I'm not." She sighed. "I'm afraid of what I'll find—or what I won't find. But there's no sense putting it off any longer." She led the way past the front door, the big brass padlock still intact, around the side of the cabin, to a big window. "This opens into the bedroom," she said, pointing up. The ground fell away sharply from the wall of the cabin, so that the window was five feet over their heads. "It's big enough to crawl through, and it's up high enough I suspect Dad didn't keep it locked, but I don't know how we're going to get up there."

"Wait a sec." Ryan hurried back toward the front of the cabin. She stuffed her hands in the pockets of her parka and studied the window, nothing visible through the glass from this angle.

Ryan returned a few moments later, carrying an aluminum ladder. "This was behind the shed," he said. "I figured your dad probably had one around." He extended the ladder and propped it against the side of the house, wedging the bottom of it in the snow. The top reached just below the window. Then he stepped back. "You should go first," he directed. "It's your dad's house."

She hesitated.

"What's the matter?" he asked. "Are you afraid of heights?"

"It's not that." She looked up again. She wasn't going to tell him the thought that had popped into her head. What if her dad was up there, dead? But that was ridiculous. He wouldn't be in the house with that big padlock on the front door. "Hold the ladder," she said, and put her foot on the bottom rung.

RYAN WATCHED DENI climb the ladder, distracted as much by the grim expression on her face as the sight of her shapely backside as she ascended. Maybe he should have offered to do this for her, but it hadn't felt right, essentially breaking into the home of a man he scarcely knew.

She reached the third-to-last rung of the ladder and steadied herself with her hands against the window. "Everything looks okay in there," she said. "Normal."

"Can you open the window?" he called up.

She shoved up, but the window didn't move. "I might need something to pry it," she said.

"Stay still," he offered. "I'll get something from the shed."

He ran to the shed and returned half a minute later with a pry bar that had hung above the workbench. "Climb down and get this," he said. "I don't think two of us on the ladder would be safe."

She climbed down a few steps, until she could reach the pry bar he held up to her. Then she hurried back to the window, and fit the narrow end of the bar under the sash. The ladder shifted as she pried at the window and he steadied it with both hands. "Careful!"

With a wrenching sound, the sash rose a couple of inches. Deni tossed down the bar and shoved the window the rest of the way up. There was no screen, so she was able to lean into the room. Then she was up and over the sill, disappearing from sight.

Seconds later, she stuck her head out and called down to him. "Do you want to come up, too?"

Not really. But it didn't seem right to have come this far only to leave her to search alone. He began climbing. He reached the top and swung his leg over the windowsill and stepped into the room. The small space—maybe eight feet by ten feet—had the stale air of a room that had been closed up and unoccupied for a while, but otherwise looked normal. A green wool blanket was pulled up over the pillow on the double bed in the corner, while a pair of jeans and a shirt were draped over the single straight-backed chair by the door. A hairbrush, coffee mug and some papers were scattered on top of a wooden dresser against the far wall. "Do you see anything unusual or out of place?" he asked.

"No, it pretty much always looks like this." She picked up a paperback book from the table beside the bed and examined it, then laid it back down. "Dad isn't much of a housekeeper."

He followed her through the open door into a larger room across the front of the cabin. A table and two chairs sat by another window on one side of the room, while two recliners, a woodstove and a lamp filled most of the rest of the space. A large braided rug, its colors mostly obscured by age or grime, covered most of the floor.

Ryan followed Deni around the room as she flipped through stacks of magazines by one of the recliners, and shuffled through another pile of papers on one end of the table. They looked like old newspapers to Ryan. "I don't know why Dad saves all this junk," she said, and picked up one of the newspapers.

"Maybe there are articles he's saving to read." He looked over her shoulder and saw the paper was folded back to a story about the ice festival, dated two weeks ago. The hair on the back of his neck rose. Jake had seemed pretty certain that Mike Traynor wasn't linked to the bomb at Caspar Canyon, but why had Mike saved an article about the festival?

Deni moved on, but Ryan flipped through the rest of the papers in the pile. Each one was folded back to an article about some new development in the county—the Nugget Hotel expansion request, the award for the highway bridge, new mining developments, new businesses that catered to tourists. If Mike was a suspect in the bombings, would these be considered evidence that he had been researching potential targets?

Deni had moved on to examining what looked like a stack of mail on the small table between the recliners. Ryan studied the rest of the room. Mike had a fondness for detective novels and spy thrillers, judging by the titles in the single bookcase against one wall. The only artwork on his walls was a watercolor of horses grazing in a meadow, mountains rising in the distance; and a shadowbox that contained a portrait of a young man in uniform; and an assortment of medals and combat patches. "Is this your dad?" he asked, studying the photo.

Deni joined him in front of the keepsake. "Yes. He was in the army during the Gulf War."

"What are the medals for?" He tilted his head, trying to read the inscriptions.

"There's a purple heart where he was wounded by shrapnel," she said. "He has a scar on his shoulder from the explosion, but he always said it was no big deal."

"This one is for marksmanship." Ryan indicated a gold shield with the image of a target. He leaned in closer to read the patch beside it. His voice trailed off, his pulse hammering in his throat as the significance of the design registered.

"What is it?" Deni leaned in beside him. "It looks like a crab."

The badge depicted a bomb over crossed lightning bolts, over two curving branches of laurel leaves. Ryan swallowed, and cleared his throat. "I'm not positive," he said. "But it says something about explosives." He looked at her, trying to gauge if the meaning behind those words had registered yet. "You said your father didn't know anything about explosives," he said. "But I think this badge says he did—that he was good enough to be awarded for his expertise."

She wet her lips. "You're saying Dad probably did know how to build a bomb?"

"Maybe." He looked at the badge again. "Maybe that's what he did in the military. Did he say?"

"No. He didn't talk about his service, and I never asked." She looked crestfallen.

"Maybe we should find out," he said.

Her eyes met his, dark and troubled. "It still doesn't prove anything."

"Of course it doesn't," he agreed. Except that her father was familiar with the places that had been targeted so far, and he may have had the skill to build a bomb. It didn't make him guilty, but they weren't finding anything to prove his innocence, either. "But I think we need to tell the sheriff about this."

"They don't think Dad did anything wrong."

"Maybe not, but they'll want to hear about this." And he couldn't in good conscience keep it a secret, now that he knew. He put his arm around her. "If you tell the sheriff's office, they can figure out if this means anything or not. If you keep the information to yourself, you could end up worrying for nothing. Or in serious trouble with the law."

"You're right." She looked around the room. "Let's go. I've seen enough."

They left, neither of them speaking on the way back to his truck. The silence continued, a heaviness in the air around them as they drove toward town. As he turned off the forest service road onto the highway, Ryan glanced at her. "Are you okay?" he asked.

She shifted toward him. "I wasn't completely honest when I said I didn't see anything out of place back there," she said.

"Oh?" He tensed. "What did you see?"

She made a fist and brought it to her mouth, as if trying to keep back the words. "Dad had a trunk in his bedroom—at the foot of his bed. The trunk isn't there."

"What was in the trunk—do you know?"

She nodded. "I don't know everything, but I do know he kept his guns there."

"What kind of guns?"

"A couple of pistols and at least one rifle. Maybe more. I didn't want to know about them, so I didn't ask. But he wouldn't have taken that trunk if he was just going out to ride his snowmobile." She let out a ragged breath. "I'm really worried. Whatever is going on with Dad, I don't think it's anything good."

Chapter Seven

For the second time in a week, Ryan found himself back at the Rayford County Sheriff's Department with Deni. Deputy Dwight Prentice was the only officer on duty when Deni and Ryan arrived Sunday afternoon. "I need to talk to someone about my father," Deni said after he met them in the front lobby. "We've just come from his cabin and I found some things the sheriff needs to know about. It may be nothing, but I think he should know."

"Come back here and tell me," Dwight said. "I'll pass it on to the sheriff."

He led them to a crowded office, cleared off two chairs for them, then listened as Deni told him about visiting her dad's cabin. "I noticed right away the trunk that usually sat at the end of his bed was missing," she said. "I was hoping he had moved it to some other part of the house, but we didn't find it."

"What about that trunk worries you?" Dwight asked.

"I know my dad kept guns in that trunk. He showed me once—there were two pistols and a rifle in there, and some ammunition and other things. I wasn't interested, so I didn't pay close attention."

"I'll pass this along to the sheriff," Dwight said. He didn't sound alarmed but then, he probably had a lot of practice not giving anything away.

"That isn't the only thing we found," she said.

"What else?" Dwight asked.

Deni looked to Ryan, who nodded in a way he hoped was encouraging. "Dad has this shadowbox on the wall, with a picture of him from when he was in the army, and some medals and stuff," she said. "My mom made it and gave it to him for Christmas one year. He's had it for years and though I've looked at it a hundred times, I never really noticed—" She glanced at Ryan. "Ryan is the one who spotted the badge in there—apparently my dad was some kind of explosives expert in the military."

Dwight tensed. "What makes you say that?"

Ryan described the badge. "I'm pretty sure it's for service in some special explosives unit," he said.

Dwight swiveled his chair to face the computer on his desk and began typing. A few moments later, he angled the screen to face them. "Is this what you saw?" he asked.

The image was of the same bomb over crossed lightning bolts, over a swag of laurel. "Yes." Deni looked from the image on the screen to Dwight. "Do you know what it is?"

"It's an explosive ordnance specialist patch," Dwight said. "If your father has this, it means he was trained to deal with the disarmament and disposal, and construction and deployment of explosives."

"I didn't know." Deni shook her head, looking stunned. "When the sheriff asked me if my dad knew about explosives, I told him he didn't. Dad was a truck driver. But I guess I was wrong. Dad never talked about his time in the army, and I never asked."

"Do you know where he served?" Dwight asked.

"He was in the Gulf War. Desert Storm?"

Dwight nodded. "We'll look into this. Will you give us permission to cut the lock on the cabin door and do a more thorough search?"

"Yes. Do you think it will help you find my father?"

"It might."

"We didn't see anything to indicate that Mike had done anything wrong," Ryan said.

Dwight nodded. "We need to check it out." He typed into the computer again, then stood and retrieved a printout from a computer nearby. "You'll need to sign this," he said, laying the single sheet of paper in front of Deni. "It gives us permission to remove the lock and search the cabin."

She signed where he indicated. "Dad is going to be really angry when he finds out I did this," she said.

"You're a loving daughter who's concerned about her father," Dwight reassured. "Let's make this more official. How long has your dad been gone now?"

"Since Wednesday before last. That's the last time I talked to him on the phone."

"Would you like to file a missing persons report on him?" Dwight asked.

Her expression brightened. "Yes!"

Dwight filled out another report and printed it for Deni to sign. "This will add resources to our search for your father," he said.

"Thank you." She stood. "You'll let me know if you find anything?"

He nodded, but Ryan wondered how much the sheriff's department would reveal, if they found anything that indicated Mike Traynor had participated in a crime. They probably wouldn't want Deni passing on that information to her father.

They left the sheriff's department. "Do you want to get coffee or something to eat?" he asked.

"I just want to go home." She gave him an apologetic look. "I'm sorry. I'm terrible company right now."

"You don't have to be any particular way with me." He unlocked the Tundra and they climbed in and drove to her house in silence. He sensed her weariness and her sadness and wished he could do something to help her.

At her house, he walked her to her door. "Thank you for coming with me today," she said.

"Are you sure you'll be all right?" he asked.

She leaned into him and his arms automatically went around her. She felt so right, close to him this way. "I don't know. I… Dad is a grown man. He can do what he wants. But…"

"But he's your father and you love him and you're worried about him," he supplied.

"Yes."

"Call me if you need anything," he said. "Or if you just need to talk." He started to step away, but she held on to him, and pressed her lips to his. The kiss had a fierce, desperate quality, as if she was trying to blot out her pain with passion. But he responded with equal fervor, willing to give comfort any way he could, and enjoying the way she made him feel. The heat of her curves against him aroused him, and he pulled her closer, savoring the taste of her, inhaling the perfume of her hair and smoothing his hand along the curve of her hip.

When at last she pulled away, he reluctantly let her go. "I'd better go," she said, and turned and ducked into the house.

He stood for a moment on the step, letting his breathing return to normal and reining in his frustration. He had prided himself on living a simple life, free of complications and any hint of trouble. But there was nothing simple about Deni or her life. Nothing simple about her missing father, who might or might not be terrorizing locals with homemade bombs. Ryan knew all the bad ways this could play out, but he couldn't stay away from her. He couldn't abandon her when she needed him. He was a strong man, but he wasn't strong enough for that.

Deni felt important, worth facing a lot of trouble for. She had shifted something inside him, something surprising, a little frightening, yet with the potential to be wonderful. As long as she would let him, he intended to stick around, to see what happened next.

MONDAY, DENI'S CLASS was scheduled to take a field trip to the Zenith Gold Mine, and she arrived at school to the chaos of excited children and anxious parents. She met up with seventh grade teacher Mallory Rush, whose class would also be part of the outing, in the gymnasium.

"Want to take bets on how many kids get carsick on the bus and who freaks out when we get down in the mine tunnel?" Mallory asked as they surveyed the milling children.

"I might freak out in the mine tunnel," Deni said. "Whose idea was this particular field trip? No one asked me."

"Zenith Gold Mine reached out to the school and offered to host classes," Mallory said. "All part of their efforts to be good local citizens. Some people weren't happy with them reopening the mine. There were concerns about traffic and the environmental impact. I guess this is their response. Besides, it meshes well with our natural science and local history curriculum." Mallory sipped her coffee. "I think it'll be interesting."

Deni tasted her own coffee—she had had just enough time to say hi and bye to Ryan as she dashed in to grab her usual latte on the way to work. But the memory of that brief exchange, pleasant as it was, wasn't enough to counter the queasiness in her stomach at the memory of her father's participation in the protests over the mine's reopening. His photo had been printed in the paper as part of a group shot taken of people picketing at the entrance to the mine. They hadn't broken any laws, but what if her father had decided to take his dislike of progress further?

"Ms. Traynor, Drake says we have to hold our breath when we get underground at the mine or we'll use up all the oxygen." Kendra Richardson, the beads on the ends of her braids rattling, skidded to a stop in front of Deni. "That's not true, is it? It can't be true."

"It's not true," Deni said. "People work in that mine all day and they certainly don't hold their breath while they're there. There's plenty of oxygen in the tunnels." She hoped. "I'm sure they pipe it in or something."

Kendra nodded, though she didn't look very relieved. Deni looked around for Drake. She suspected the boy, who had a reputation for stirring up trouble, had a crush on Kendra and was trying to impress her. Most boys his age didn't seem to grasp that the way to a girl's heart did not lie in frightening her or grossing her out.

"Our bus is here!" someone shouted, which started a mass push toward the exit.

"Everyone line up!" Mallory called.

"Eighth graders, over here by me," Deni called. "Adam, that means you, too," she added as Adam Escovar veered off toward the back exit.

When she was sure everyone was ushered safely onto the bus, she took a seat beside Marsha Edmonds at the front of the vehicle. Marsha's daughter Sadie was one of six children, and Marsha volunteered with all their classes, so that she spent as much time at the school as some of the teachers. "How are you doing, Marsha?" Deni asked as the bus moved forward.

"I'm good. I'm sorry to hear about your dad, though."

"My dad?" Deni didn't try to hide her alarm.

"I heard he was missing. I saw a notice on the bulletin board at the post office."

Deni immediately felt guilty. The sheriff's department must have posted the notice, but why hadn't she thought of that? Should she print posters with her dad's picture to hand out? It was what people did for missing children and dogs, but did it apply to a fifty-five-year-old who may have left of his own accord?

Marsha was still looking at her, so she forced a response. "Thanks. He's probably fine, but it's not really like him to go off without saying anything to me."

"I saw him in the hardware store week before last," Marsha said. "He was buying a bunch of wire, I guess for some electrical work at his cabin. You can run everything off solar these days, can't you?"

"I guess so," Deni said. Dad had never mentioned any work on the cabin to her. She thought she knew everything about his life—how wrong she had been.

As the bus drove onto the bridge across Grizzly Creek she shuddered, remembering the mock rescue. There had been the same kind of excitement as today in the run-up to that exercise. Getting made up to look injured and practicing what they would say and do had been fun.

Then the rescue workers had found the bomb wired to the bridge and she had been hit with the realization of how close they had been to true danger.

A few minutes later the bus stopped at the entrance to the Zenith Gold Mine. A man in a hard hat came out from a guardhouse and climbed onto the bus. "Welcome to Zenith Mines," he said in a hearty voice. "Today you're going to see how a modern-day gold mine works. You'll see some things most people never get to see."

"If we find some gold, can we keep it?" one of the seventh graders asked.

"That depends on where you find it," the man said. "After lunch, you can try your hand at panning for gold in the creek, just like the pioneers did. You can keep any gold you find then."

A flurry of excited conversation drowned out whatever he was going to say next. Deni rose and faced the rest of the bus. "We're going to stay on this bus until everyone is quiet," she said.

The silence wasn't instant, but things did quiet down considerably. The man in the hard hat—who introduced himself as Kent—continued.

"The Zenith was founded in 1887 by Philemon Cass, a speculator from Boston who came to these mountains looking for gold. Where a lot of people who had the same idea failed, Phil succeeded, and discovered the rich vein of gold and other precious metals that we are still harvesting from today."

Kent shared a little more of the history of the mine as the children fidgeted. Deni, who had sat again, sent him a look meant to signal he should move things along before boredom overcame manners and the students started talking over him again.

Thankfully, he wrapped up his spiel about history and said, "Are you ready to go down into the mine?"

"Yes!" rang out a chorus of voices.

"No!" added several more.

"How will we get there?" someone asked.

"You'll ride a train." Kent grinned as several children responded with excited whoops. He looked to Deni. "Are you ready?"

She nodded and stood once more. "All right. Everyone off the bus in an orderly fashion. Stay together and follow Kent's instructions."

"As you exit the bus each one of you will be given a hard hat and a yellow slicker," Kent said. "Put these on, then follow Ben, who will have a hard hat like mine." He pointed to the yellow safety helmet he was wearing. "He'll lead you to the train."

They managed to get everyone off the bus and outfitted with hard hats and slickers, including all the adults. "What's the raincoat for?" Sadie Edmonds asked.

"It can be wet down in the mine," Kent explained.

The train that would convey them into the mine consisted of three open cars attached to an electric tractor. Kent ran through safety precautions, including "keep your hands and heads inside the car at all times" which at least half a dozen boys immediately ignored.

But at last they were off, traveling from daylight into darkness—but only briefly, as bright lights banished every shadow from the rest of the tunnel. "You can't even tell we're really underground," one girl observed, and Deni had to agree—they might have been inside any windowless museum, except that the walls, ceilings and floors of this place were all made of gray rock.

The company had obviously put a lot of thought into this tour. The tram stopped briefly in a large space set up to look like a historical mine, complete with mannequins in old-fashioned clothing holding pickaxes and sticks of what she hoped was fake dynamite. Kent explained how early miners used the dynamite to break rock loose from the sides of the tunnels, then hauled the rock in handcarts to the surface, to be sorted for transport to the mill, where the valuable minerals could be extracted. He answered the children's questions about the process, though Abigail Murphy flummoxed him when she asked why all the mannequins had funny moustaches.

"That's so they can strain their soup!" Drake called, sending the group of boys around him into gales of laughter, while the girls rolled their eyes.

The tram started up again and they moved into a more modern section of the mine, with pneumatic lines running along the ceiling, safety posters on the wall and men and machinery all around. Kent rattled off statistics about the amount of ore taken from the mine daily and projected earnings, but the children seemed content to watch the men—and as far as Deni could tell, they were all men—work.

Deni sat back, feeling more relaxed now. Her father would have loved this, she thought, both the historical aspect and the glimpse of the modern operation. He had always loved learning things, and he and her mother had passed that love on to her. Had that aspect of his personality really changed?

She estimated they had been in the mine about an hour and a half when Kent announced they would head back up top. "You can have lunch in our outdoor pavilion, then pan for gold in the creek. How does that sound?"

The students'—and possibly some of the parents'—cheers echoed off the stone walls. The train started backward down the tunnel. Kent leaned over Deni's seat and whispered. "Don't worry—we salt the creek with flakes of real gold for the kids to find," he said. "And a lot of chunks of iron pyrite, which most of them seem to like just as much."

"You've done a wonderful job with the tour," she said. "Thank you so much."

Their exit was much faster than the trip down, the tram traveling surprisingly fast through the tunnel. Deni felt a little dizzy, but welcomed the idea that they would soon be back up top in the open air.

She could see the entrance up ahead, an oval of light past the brief stretch of unlit tunnel. She was focused on this, and mentally running through the procedure for distributing sack lunches to the students, when the tram lurched.

"What was that?" a girl asked.

"These old trams are balky sometimes," Kent said. He turned, as if to address Ben, who was driving the tractor.

Later, Deni couldn't remember the order in which everything happened. In her memory, the darkness descended first, then the explosion and dust. She was falling, the tram cars tossed onto their sides, and screaming filled the air. Not the overly dramatic wails of the mock rescue, but true cries of terror, both her own and those of the children. Children who were hurt and needed her help.

Chapter Eight

Ryan was at work when he received the text from search and rescue. The words on the screen sent a shock wave through him: Explosion at Zenith Mine. A number of children and adults trapped/injured. Urgent.

His boss's eyes widened when Ryan showed him the text. "Kids? What were they doing up at the mine?"

"I don't know," Ryan said. "But I need to go. They'll need everyone they can get on this rescue."

"Of course," he said. He made a shooing motion. "Go!"

Ryan kept his gear in his truck. He pulled on his parka as he drove, and fell into a line of vehicles headed toward the mine—sheriff's and fire department vehicles and ambulances, the cars of other first responders and probably media and concerned or curious civilians. He tried to envision what he might find at the mine.

But his imagination didn't prepare him for the chaos he drove into just past the entrance gates. A sheriff's department vehicle blocked the road a quarter mile from the gate, but waved Ryan through when he saw the search and rescue parka. Ryan left his truck behind

Sheri Stevens's Jeep, grabbed his pack and jogged to the Beast, where the rest of the search and rescue team was gathering.

Tony, grim-faced, stood with a man in a yellow hard hat. "This is Peter Grayson, with Zenith Mines," Tony said. "He's going to give us a rundown on the situation."

Grayson, his face the color of paste, nodded. "The tram with the kids was at the entrance to the mine when the explosion occurred," he said. "One car was mostly out of the tunnel, but the explosion twisted the tram tracks and threw the cars over onto their sides. Some of the kids and adults were able to walk away, but we know others are trapped under the tram cars or under rock that fell as a result of the explosion."

"How many kids and adults?" Tony asked.

"Forty-seven total," Grayson said. "We don't know how many made it out and how many are still trapped. There are two mine employees with them. We were able to evacuate the rest of our employees through emergency exits."

"Why were the kids there?" Sheri asked.

"Field trip, from Eagle Mountain Middle School," Grayson said.

Ryan's heart stopped for half a second, then began beating so hard it hurt. "What classes?" he asked. "What grade?"

"Seventh and eighth," Grayson said.

"Do we know the cause of the explosion?" Ted, who was standing just behind Ryan, asked.

"No," Grayson said.

"Some buildup of gas in the mine or something like that?" Eldon asked.

"No." Grayson shook his head. "That can't happen. Not with the ventilation system we have. And not at the mine entrance."

"Sabotage?" Danny asked.

"We're not going to speculate at this time," Grayson said.

"That's not our concern," Tony said. He stepped forward and began assigning jobs and distributing gear.

The team headed toward the mine entrance. As they drew nearer they could see the tram car on its side amid a tumble of rock, other emergency personnel already working to shift rock and tend to the injured. Paramedics, including some SAR volunteers, worked on the injured, while Ryan and others began the search for more survivors, and for those who had not been so lucky.

"Deni Traynor is here somewhere," he said to no one in particular. "Let me know if you find her."

Soon all his attention was focused on freeing a little girl from beneath the tram. Miraculously, she was wedged in a gap between two boulders and other than a scrape on one arm and a terrible fright, was unharmed. He sent her off in the care of a female firefighter and turned his attention to an adult, who proved to be the seventh-grade teacher, Mallory Rush. Mallory had twisted her knee, but was calm. "Who is the other teacher with you?" Ryan asked as he and Ted shifted the rocks around her. He already knew the answer, but he wanted confirmation.

"Deni Traynor," Mallory said. "She's in the first car.

The one farthest in the mine." She bit her lip, which had begun to tremble.

A front-end loader rumbled up, a man in coveralls and a hard hat at the controls. "We need to shift the rock blocking the entrance to get at the others," he shouted over the rumble of the diesel engine.

Grayson jogged up to them. "We've established radio contact with one of the workers inside," he said. "They've got some injured kids and one adult who was hit in the head by a rock and unconscious, but the car protected them from most of the rock fall."

"Who is the adult?" Ryan asked. He had a horrible image of Deni lying among the rock, senseless.

Grayson shook his head. "I don't know. A woman."

Ryan felt sick, but pushed the nausea aside. He retreated with the other volunteers while the front-end loader operator and other mine workers began the slow process of carefully shifting the cascade of rock and debris.

It took over an hour to move most of the rock. Meanwhile, they evacuated the children and adults in the first tram car. Three people had to be transported by ambulance with broken bones, but all of the injured were expected to recover.

As the pile of debris blocking the mine tunnel diminished, the rescuers waiting outside could hear sobs and cries from those trapped inside. Ryan bit the inside of his cheek to keep from shouting Deni's name. Even if she could hear him, he wouldn't be able to help her. Not yet.

"A little different from that mock rescue, huh?" Eldon said.

Ryan nodded. No training exercise could prepare you for the reality of an actual event, in which people were seriously injured or possibly dying. And no one talked much about the feeling of helplessness that flooded him now, as they waited for someone else to make it possible to do the jobs they had trained for.

At last, the machinery and men cleared a pathway into the mine. Rescuers swarmed into the tunnel, like soldiers charging into battle.

Ryan headed toward the front of the tram. "Hello!" he shouted. "I'm with search and rescue. Who's here?"

A chorus of voices answered. "We're in the tram car," said a strong male voice.

Rescuers had to climb on top of the car and squeeze between the rock wall of the tunnels and the edge of the open tram car. Ryan dropped down into a scene eerily reminiscent of the mock bus crash—a vehicle on its side, children and adults clustered in twos and threes in an upside-down world.

Except that this scene was dark, save for dim emergency lights on the tram and the puddles of light from the rescuers' headlamps, and the blood that smeared children's faces and bodies was real, not corn syrup and food coloring.

"We need to move everyone to the end of the car," a fireman instructed Ryan. "We've got a torch to cut away the side of the tram car to make evacuating everyone a little easier."

Ryan found Deni in the crush at the end of the car.

She had a streak of dirt or grease across her cheek, but seemed otherwise unharmed. "Are you okay?" he asked, examining her face for any sign of pain.

"I'm fine," she said.

"They told us a woman had a head injury and was unconscious," he said. "I was so afraid it was you."

"One of the chaperones, Marsha Edmonds." She turned to look at where nurse Danny Irwin was examining a brunette in jeans and a blue sweater. "I hope she's okay."

Ryan put his arm around Deni and held her as the whine of the torch drowned out further conversation. A few moments later a shout went up and light from a powerful work lamp bathed the space.

Ted stood up and took charge. "Everyone who can walk unaided, line up and follow Deputy Douglas here."

Deputy Jamie Douglas waved from the new opening. "Come on, everybody," she said. "Let's get out of here."

"I should go with my students," Deni said, and moved out of Ryan's arms.

He nodded. He had work of his own to do here. Now that he knew she was safe, he felt lighter, more focused on the job at hand.

Ryan lost track of how long he and the other rescuers worked, performing triage, stabilizing limbs, preparing patients for transport and searching for anyone who might have been left behind. By the time they received the message to stand down and emerged from the tunnel, he was surprised to see the light was fading.

Much of the crowd that had been in the area earlier

had dispersed. Parents had long since come to claim children, the ambulances had transported the more seriously injured, and only a few sheriff's deputies and firefighters remained, along with a contingent of mine workers.

The search and rescue team convened once more at the Beast to load in equipment and review the operation. "The forty-seven people on the tram were all accounted for," Tony said, consulting the notes he had made on a tablet. "Twelve children with minor injuries. One adult with a concussion, admitted to the hospital for observation. Five children with broken bones, two with cuts severe enough to require stitches, one crushed finger which I'm told should heal." He looked up. "The fact that they were all wearing hard hats, and that they were at the mine entrance when the explosion occurred, saved a lot of lives today."

"What caused the explosion?" Ted asked. "Was it another bomb, like the one at Caspar Canyon?"

"The sheriff's department and mine officials aren't saying anything yet," Tony said.

Ted grunted.

"Good job today," Tony said. "Let's get back to headquarters and put away the gear, then go home and get some rest."

Ryan started toward his truck. He was surprised to find Deputy Jake Gwynn waiting for him. "Have you spoken with Deni today?" Jake asked before Ryan could ask him what he wanted.

"I saw her in the mine, briefly." Ryan took out his

keys and pressed the button on the fob to unlock the truck. "She was in the first car, but she's okay. Why?"

"We're wondering if she's heard anything from her father."

"She would have told the sheriff's department if she had." Ryan slipped off his pack and stuffed it into the back of the truck. "What's going on? Was that explosion caused by another bomb?"

Jake looked grim. "I can't say."

"Which makes me believe it was. That, and you're looking for Mike Traynor. If you haven't seen him, Deni hasn't, either."

"He's her father," Jake said. "It would be natural for her to want to protect him."

"She's worried about him and she wants to find him," Ryan countered. "That doesn't mean she's going to condone him doing anything wrong." He faced the deputy, one hand on the door of the truck, a sudden wave of emotion making him shake. "She could have been killed today. Do you think Mike would put his own daughter in danger like that?"

"He probably didn't know about the field trip," Jake said.

"Did you find anything at his cabin?" Ryan asked.

"We were on our way there when we got the call about the explosion," Jake told him.

"Then you don't have anything to tie Mike to this bomb," Ryan said. "And you certainly can't link Deni to it."

"We're not saying Deni is involved," Jake said.

Ryan noticed he didn't try to deny that the explosion had been caused by another bomb. "If you want to talk to Deni, talk to her," he advised. "I don't have anything to tell you that she wouldn't."

Jake stepped back. "Tell Deni if she hears anything, to contact us right away," he said.

"You tell her," Ryan stated. He got in the truck and slammed the door. He needed to stop by SAR headquarters and help with the gear. Then all he wanted was to go back to his place, have a beer and something to eat and try to block out this nightmare of a day with some mindless TV.

But first, he had to see Deni. If he was feeling wrecked by the day, she must feel even worse. And no one should have to go through that alone.

Chapter Nine

"It's a bomb."

"A bomb."

"It must have been a bomb."

Deni heard the conversation around her as she huddled in the overturned tram car with her students, and later, as she waited in the area outside the mine entrance until she was certain all her students were accounted for. Officials refused to confirm these suspicions, but the bombing at Caspar Canyon and the attempt to destroy the Grizzly Creek bridge had everyone convinced that a terrorist was targeting their little community.

All Deni could think of was her father protesting the reopening of the mine. And him buying electrical wire at the hardware store shortly before he disappeared. *That doesn't prove anything,* she told herself. But it didn't make him appear innocent either, did it?

She had been home about an hour and had just stepped out of the shower when her doorbell rang. She hurried to finish drying off and pulled on her robe, then, in bare feet, went to see who was calling.

Ryan stood on the front porch, still in his SAR parka. She pulled open the door. "Ryan?"

His gaze flicked over her, heat behind the look, and she was conscious of being naked beneath the robe—even though it was an ankle-length plush model that revealed nothing save a triangle of damp skin at the base of her throat and her bare toes.

"Can I come in?" he asked.

"Sure." She stepped back and he moved past her into the front room. He smelled like fresh air and woodsmoke and the faintest hint of aftershave, a combination that struck her as sexy, though maybe it wasn't the scent so much as the man himself.

She shut the door and he turned to her. "You look like you're feeling a little better," he said. "At least you're not as pale."

She tucked a lock of damp hair behind one ear. "I was terrified," she said. "It was bad enough going into that mine and being underground, but being trapped in that overturned tram car, not knowing if we were buried under tons of rock, or if there would be more explosions…" She hugged her arms across her stomach, queasy at the memory. "The only thing that helped me keep it together was knowing the kids needed me." She met his gaze again. "No one was seriously hurt, were they? I was told everybody would be okay, but I wasn't sure if they had found everyone at that point."

"There are a couple of broken bones, and a parent with a concussion, but they should all recover." He touched her shoulder lightly. "Let's sit down."

"Marsha Edmonds's hard hat must have come off

when the tram car overturned," Deni said as he steered her toward the sofa. "She was sitting right next to me. At first, I didn't know where she was or what had happened to her. I didn't know where anyone was. Then someone switched on some emergency lighting in the tram car. It was still dim, but when I saw all the blood and she wouldn't answer me, I was so afraid she was going to die."

"She's in the hospital but the word we got is that she's going to be okay."

They sat and Ryan took her hand. "Do you want to talk about what happened, or would you rather not?"

"The tour was almost over. I could see the mine entrance up ahead. Then everything went crazy. I can't... I can't even explain. One minute we were riding in the car and the next we were lying sort of under it. There were loud noises and smoke and darkness, children screaming, blood..." She shuddered. "I thought we were all going to die."

He pulled her close and she laid her head on his shoulder and closed her eyes. This was what she needed, just to be held.

"You're okay now," he said, his voice soft and soothing.

"It was the oddest sensation." She opened her eyes, but didn't lift her head from his shoulder. "All day I had flashes of having been through this before—déjà vu. I think it was the mock bus wreck I participated in the week before. The scenario had so many similarities. Was it like that for you, too?"

"We knew going in that the bus wreck wasn't real,

even though we tried hard to act as if it was." He smoothed his hand down her shoulder. "It's so different in a real emergency. It was dark, and there was a lot of debris. We weren't sure where everyone was, and we had to wait a long time for mine personnel and machinery to dig out the tunnel so we could reach the injured."

"I only saw one small part of the whole scene," she said. "And that was terrifying enough."

"At first it looked much worse than it turned out to be," Ryan added. "Someone said that the fact you were all wearing hard hats probably saved lives, and when the cars were thrown over on their sides, they shielded you from the worst of the blast."

"Right away I heard people say it was a bomb." The thought made her feel sick. "I guess with what happened in Caspar Canyon and at the Grizzly Creek bridge, that was on everyone's mind."

"No one is saying yet exactly what caused the explosion," Ryan said. "They probably don't know yet. Mines still use explosives to get at the ore, don't they? And there could be pockets of gas trapped underground, I think."

She sat up straighter and stared at him. "Do you mean it might not be a bomb at all?"

"I don't know," he said.

The sob that escaped her startled her. She covered her mouth with both hands, trying to stifle it, but the tears flowed freely. Ryan put his arm around her again. "It's okay," he soothed.

She shook her head. It—whatever "it" was—was not okay, but she appreciated him wanting to comfort her. Her feelings were in such turmoil. "I want to believe my dad doesn't have anything to do with any of these explosions," she said. "But I keep remembering things or hearing things that seem incriminating—even though I know they may not mean anything."

"What kind of things?" he asked.

She plucked at the lapel of the robe, a nervous gesture. "Marsha and I were talking and she told me she had seen my dad at the hardware store about two weeks ago. She said he was buying electrical wire. But why would he do that? His cabin doesn't have electricity. So I thought, maybe bombs need electrical wire for something."

Ryan frowned. "The only explosives I've been around are the ones the highway department uses to trigger avalanches to keep the roads clear. They use charges that explode on impact, so, like grenades or rockets. No electrical wire." He shrugged. "I guess you could look it up online."

"I don't think I want that on my browsing history," she said.

"Your dad was probably just doing some work for a friend or something," Ryan said.

But what friend? How terrible was it that she didn't even know who he socialized with when he wasn't with her.

"What else are you worried about?" he asked.

"Dad hated that they reopened the Zenith Mine," she said. "He was one of the people who tried to block the opening. They filed papers in court and when that didn't work they picketed the site and tried to block work on the mine."

"I remember people were worried about environmental damage," Ryan said. "But so far I take it the mining company is doing a good job."

"They seem to be," she said. "When we were on the tour today, I remember thinking that Dad would have really enjoyed it. They had a section on the history of the mine, and the demonstration of the extraction methods they use today was really interesting."

"It seemed to me there was a lot of security at the mine," Ryan said. "I don't see how anyone who didn't work there could possibly get into the mine to plant a bomb."

She stared at him. "I hadn't thought of that."

"I don't see how your father could have anything to do with what happened at the mine," Ryan said. "And no matter what he thought about the mine, surely he wouldn't put you and a bunch of students in danger."

"He didn't know about the field trip," she said. "Or at least, he and I never talked about it. We didn't talk about my work much."

"He wasn't interested?" Ryan asked.

"It wasn't that. But my mom was a teacher and hearing about my job was just one more reminder she isn't around anymore." She swallowed a fresh knot of tears and took a deep breath. "But you're right. He wouldn't have wanted to hurt me, or children." Surely, he wouldn't. She leaned against him once more. "All this worrying is exhausting. I wish I knew what the sheriff's department found at Dad's cabin. You and I didn't really see anything, but do you think they found something suspicious?"

"I ran into Deputy Jake Gwynn at the mine site this afternoon," Ryan said. "He told me they were on their way to search Mike's cabin when they got the call about the explosion at the mine. So I guess they haven't gotten up there yet."

She sighed. "So we wait a little longer."

"Jake told me to tell you to contact them if you heard from your dad."

"Does he think I won't?"

He looked pained. "You need to know that whenever someone is suspected of a crime like this, law enforcement looks at all the people around them, friends and family. If your father has done something wrong and authorities think you helped him, you could end up in trouble, too."

"But I haven't done anything wrong." She stared at him, heart racing. "You believe me, don't you?"

He squeezed her hand. "I believe you. I'm just telling you how law enforcement works, so you can be prepared."

"How do you know this?"

He looked down at their clasped hands. "I've known people who have had to deal with this kind of thing."

"This whole situation is so bizarre," she said.

"It is. And I don't want to see you hurt."

"I need to talk to Dad," she said. "I'm sure he could explain everything."

"I think it would be better if you let law enforcement handle this," Ryan said.

"He's my father. I can't abandon him."

He released her hand and sat back. "Okay. But if you're going to find your dad, you have to be smart about it. You said you last spoke to your dad Wednesday almost two weeks ago, right? And you saw him at the town council meeting last Wednesday."

"Then you do believe it was him I saw?"

"Of course." He said it so matter-of-factly, but relief flooded her. She had been worried that he would think she was overreacting, seeing her father in places where he wasn't.

"Anyway," he continued. "That means wherever he's hiding, he's not that far away. He has his truck with the camper, his snowmobile on a trailer and probably other stuff."

A trunk of guns, she thought, but said nothing.

"To me, that suggests he's camping, probably in the mountains," Ryan said.

She nodded. "He liked to camp. Even in winter. But the sheriff's department will have figured this out, too, won't they? They're probably looking for him."

"I'm not so sure they are. They said Mike wasn't very high on their suspect list, and even though you filed a missing persons report, Rayford County has a small force. With the bombs, and now the explosion at the Zenith Mine, they don't have the time or personnel to do a very widespread search."

"So what do you suggest?" she asked.

He hesitated. "The two of us could drive around some. We can visit some likely camping locations and see if we can find any indication that your dad has been there. Maybe we'd get really lucky and even find him."

She tried to tamp down the hope that soared at his words, but the idea of doing something—anything—to help her father made her feel lighter.

"That's a fabulous idea." She slipped her arms around him and hugged him close. He returned the embrace, his gaze dropping to where her robe had spread a little farther apart, revealing the curve of her breasts. Once more, she was aware of how little she was wearing, but she didn't pull away.

Instead, she slid one hand up, fingers twining in his hair, and urged his face down toward hers.

They kissed slowly, as if they had all the time in the world to explore the sensation of warm lips meeting, mouths open, tongues tangling. He broke the kiss. "Maybe we shouldn't be doing this," he said.

"Why not?" She angled toward him, letting the robe fall open a little wider. "I really like you," she said. "And I really want you."

She sighed as he cupped her breast. "Yeah. I want you, too." He dragged one thumb across her hardened nipple.

She squirmed, bringing him closer still. The robe was all the way open now, and she brought her right leg up to drape her thigh across his. A draft swept across her crotch, and she thought of Ryan touching her there, and bit back a moan.

He was caressing her bare bottom now, stroking down and around to her thigh, fingertips tantalizingly close to her sex, his lips trailing kisses along her jaw, then down the side of her neck. She tilted her head to provide him better access, as he reached down to unfasten his belt.

The sound of the doorbell pierced her like a jolt of electricity. She stared up at Ryan, confused, as it sounded again.

He swore and withdrew his hands from beneath her robe. "Are you expecting someone?"

"No." The bell sounded again, followed by a hard knocking.

"You'd better answer it," Ryan said.

She stood and cinched the robe tighter, then walked to the door, Ryan right behind her.

Two men she didn't recognize stood in the yellow glow of the porch light. Ryan looked at her. She shook her head. "I've never seen them before," she whispered.

"Ms. Traynor, open the door please," one of the men said. "We need to talk to you."

"Who are you?" she asked.

"We're with the United States Bureau of Alcohol, Tobacco, Firearms and Explosives. We need to talk to you about your father."

Chapter Ten

Ryan took an immediate dislike to the two men who strode into Deni's living room, partly because they had interrupted his make-out session with her, and partly because of the way the taller of the two looked Deni up and down, the way a hungry dog might size up a steak. "Sorry to interrupt your evening," the man said, in a voice that made it clear he wasn't sorry at all.

"Who are you?" Ryan asked. They had flashed a couple of official-looking badges on the front porch, but he had no idea what those badges had said.

"Who are you?" the shorter man, with buzz-cut blond hair and a cocky swagger, demanded.

While the feds glared at Ryan, Deni stepped forward. "I'd like to see those IDs again," she said.

With exaggerated slowness, the tall man—slicked back hair and cowboy boots with pointed toes—fished a wallet from the inside pocket of his black overcoat and opened it. "Agent Olivera, United States Bureau of Alcohol, Tobacco, Firearms and Explosives," he said.

"Agent Ferris." The blond offered his own wallet.

Deni nodded. "You can wait here while I get dressed," she said.

"Ma'am, you need to stay here where we can see you," Olivera instructed.

Deni lifted her chin and sent him a look that should have had frost forming on his eyebrows. "I'm not going to talk to you until I'm dressed." Not waiting for an answer, she turned and left the room.

Ferris made a move as if to follow, but Ryan blocked his path. "She didn't have to let you in," Ryan said. "You can wait a few more minutes."

Instead of answering, Ferris turned and began examining the room.

"What's your relationship to Ms. Traynor?" Olivera asked.

"A friend," Ryan said.

"Your name?"

"Ryan Welch."

"Do you know Mike Traynor?" Olivera asked.

"No."

Ferris picked up a framed photograph of Deni with her father. The two of them were standing on a mountain summit against a backdrop of clear blue sky. They had their arms around each other and grinned into the camera. They both looked so happy. "Yet you're friends with his daughter," Ferris said.

"She's not sixteen. She doesn't need her dad's permission to socialize with anyone."

"When was the last time you saw Mike Traynor?" Olivera asked.

"I didn't."

For the next long minute the two held a staring contest. Ryan refused to be intimidated by this stranger, and held his gaze until Deni returned. She entered the room on a wave of vanilla-and-spice perfume. She had not only dressed in slacks and a soft-looking cream-colored sweater, she had dried her hair and darkened her lashes and lips. She looked less fragile than she had before.

"What can I do for you?" she asked.

"We need to ask you about your father," Olivera said.

"Why are you interested in my father?"

"Let's sit down." Olivera nodded to the sofa.

Deni sat on the sofa. Ryan settled in next to her, resisting the urge to take her hand. Gone was the weeping woman of earlier. Now she projected the dignity and strength of someone who didn't need to lean on anyone.

Olivera took the only other chair in the room, leaving Ferris to carry in a chair from the kitchen table. "We're investigating the explosion at the Zenith Mine," Olivera said.

Deni said nothing, letting the silence fill the room like poison gas.

Olivera frowned. "When was the last time you spoke to your father?" he asked.

"Have you spoken with the sheriff's department?" she asked.

"I don't think that's relevant," Olivera said.

"If you had spoken to them, you would know I haven't heard from my father since Wednesday, March 10," she said. "I reported him missing."

"You also indicated you suspected your father might

have had something to do with the bombs placed at the Grizzly Creek bridge and in the Caspar Canyon ice-climbing area," Olivera said.

So they had spoken to the sheriff, if they knew that.

"I don't know where my father is or what he's done," Deni said. "If you've read my statement to the sheriff, then you know everything I have to say."

"You were at the mine today," Ferris said.

Her gaze flickered to him. "Yes. I was there with my class of eighth graders for a field trip."

"Did your father give you anything to take with you?" Olivera asked. "Maybe he asked you to leave a package near the mine entrance."

Ryan sat forward, fists clenched on his knees. This is what he had warned her about. She had fallen under suspicion simply because she was Mike Traynor's daughter.

"I haven't seen or spoken to my father in almost two weeks," she said. "He didn't know about the field trip. And the idea that you think I would in any way endanger children—not to mention myself—is absurd."

The two agents exchanged looks Ryan couldn't interpret.

"Can you tell us anything about the explosion at the mine?" Olivera asked.

"It was terrifying," she said. "I thought we were all going to die." Her voice trembled on the last words.

"You told the sheriff your father's guns are missing," Olivera said. "What kinds of guns?"

She repeated what she had told Deputy Prentice— that she didn't know what kind of guns.

Olivera and Ferris took turns peppering her with

questions. Why had she gone to her father's cabin? What did she expect to find there? Had her father ever made threats toward the mine?

"Not threats," she said. "He protested against the mine reopening, but that was always peacefully."

"How did he protest?" Ferris asked.

"He spoke out against the reopening of the mine at a public meeting. He picketed outside the mine gates. He carried a sign with the word *reopening* in a red circle with a line drawn through it."

"Did he have any friends who worked at the mine?" Olivera asked.

"I don't know."

She didn't know where her father had gone. She thought he had bought the dynamite to get rid of a dam in the spring above his house. She hadn't known he had been trained to handle explosives in the army. She didn't know his friends.

"Were you aware your father had a criminal record?" Olivera asked.

Ryan felt the shock wave pass through Deni. Her eyes widened. "No! That isn't true."

"It's true," Ferris said, sounding smug.

Deni looked to Olivera. "What did he do? When?"

"In 1992 he was convicted of assault for beating a man in a fight in a bar. He served three months in the county jail."

"That was before I was born."

"It shows he's capable of violence," Olivera said.

"You probably carry a gun," Deni said. "I imagine you're capable of violence, too."

Olivera didn't flinch. "What about you?" he asked. "Are you capable of violence?"

To Ryan, she looked angry enough to strike the agent at the moment, but she only said, "No. I teach children for a living. I'm trying to make the world better for them, not more violent."

"So you don't have any idea what your father's plans are?"

She stood. Ryan rose also. "You're repeating yourself now," she said. "I've had an exhausting day. You can go now."

Olivera and Ferris both stood. "We're not done yet," Olivera said.

"But I am." She turned and left the room.

The muscles in Olivera's jaw bunched. "You need to tell your girlfriend she could land in serious trouble for failing to cooperate with federal authorities," he said.

"You tell her," Ryan said.

Ferris took a step toward him. Ryan tensed. He didn't relish fighting this man, but he was prepared to defend himself, and to defend Deni.

"We'll be talking to you both again," Olivera said.

The two agents walked to the door. As soon as they were gone, Ryan locked it behind them, then went in search of Deni.

DENI SAT ON the side of her bed, hands clasped between her knees, trying to stop shaking.

A knock sounded on the bedroom door. "They're gone," Ryan said. "Is it okay if I come in?"

"Please."

He came and sat beside her. "They think my father had something to do with the bomb at the mine," she said. "They think I helped them." The implication in their questions had been clear.

"They were fishing, trying to unsettle you," Ryan explained.

"I wish I had never said anything to the sheriff."

"You did the right thing," he said.

She leaned against him, and he put his arm around her shoulder. She wanted this day to be over, for none of this—not the bombs, not her father disappearing, not federal agents questioning her—to have ever happened. She knew that wasn't possible, but maybe it would be possible for just a little while to forget. To focus on something else.

She turned toward him and kissed him, intent on recapturing the passion that had flared between them before Agents Olivera and Ferris had interrupted them.

"You've had a terrible day," Ryan said. "You don't have to do this just because it's what I want."

"It's what I want," she said. "It's what I need." She crawled into his lap, and slid her hands beneath his fleece top. It felt so good to give vent to the storm of emotions swirling inside her, to surrender to good sensations instead of bad ones. He shucked off the fleece and she licked her way across the top of his shoulder, savoring the taste of him. His muscles contracted as she brushed her fingers across the hot skin of his ridged abdomen, and pleasure rippled through her as he stripped off her shirt and bra and shaped his mouth to her breast.

She traced the scar down his arm, ridged white against his skin. "Does it hurt?" she asked.

"Not much."

She dropped her hand lower, down his ribs to his pants, where she lowered the zipper of his jeans and cupped his erection. "How about that?" she murmured.

"That doesn't hurt at all." He put his hand over hers. "Before we go much further, do you have a condom?"

"I do." She hoped that was right. It had been a while since she had needed one. She slid off his lap and hurried into the bathroom. She found the box at the back of the cabinet and fished out a foil packet. She caught sight of herself in the mirror when she shut the cabinet door—cheeks flushed, eyes bright, hair curling around her chin. Not too shabby.

She decided to speed things up a little, and returned to the bedroom holding the condom packet and wearing nothing but a pair of dangling silver earrings. Cool air caressed her skin, but the chill vanished as his heated gaze swept over her.

He undressed and joined her under the covers. His clothing had hidden a lot, she decided. He had a climber's lean body with defined muscles, and he moved with fluid grace. She caressed his shoulder, and smoothed her hand down his arm. "I couldn't stop thinking about you, the first time I saw you," she said.

"Why was that?" he asked.

"You looked different." How could she explain? "Not shy, exactly, but not so, I don't know, sure of yourself. Too many of the guys I meet around here have this attitude like any woman should be thrilled to be noticed by them."

"Most of that attitude is an act," he said. "We're all scared to death of rejection." He grasped her hip and tugged her a little closer. "I noticed you, too. I thought you were out of my league."

A snort of laughter escaped before she could suppress it. "Why would you think that?"

"You were wearing expensive boots and had a nice manicure."

"So you thought I was high-maintenance."

"Nothing wrong with that, but those women usually aren't the type to be interested in a lowly laborer."

"The boots were a gift and I do my own nails." Her hand went to his erection again. "And there's nothing lowly about you."

He grinned, and rolled her onto her back, then reached for the condom.

She pulled him to her and welcomed him in, eager to know every inch of him. It took them a few moments to find a rhythm, the awkwardness smoothed by laughter, then banished by the need to be closer, to feel more.

She loved touching him, and loved the way he touched her. She lost herself in the moment, and when she tensed and bowed in the throes of her climax she shouted for joy that the grief and anguish of the day had, at least momentarily, been banished by so much good.

They clung together for a long time afterward, her face pressed to his chest, breathing in his scent, the steady thud of his heart in her ears. She thought he might have fallen asleep when he stirred and stroked his hand down her shoulder. "You're amazing—you know that?" he said.

"Mmm." She snuggled down closer, hoping to drift off to sleep, but she should have known thoughts of the day wouldn't stay away long. She opened her eyes and shifted until she could see his face. "Did you mean that, about going to look for my dad?"

"Yes. Whenever you want."

"Friday. School is out. Do you have to work?"

"I'll get off."

So there was that to look forward to—or to dread. The shock of learning her dad had been in jail came back to her, though not as terrible now. "I never knew Dad had been in jail," she said.

"I guess it's not the kind of thing a parent tells his kid. But it sounds like he did his time and never stepped out of line again. There are probably a lot of people like that."

"Did you ever get in a fight?" she asked. "Actually hit someone?"

"I think I threatened some guy who ticked me off in a bar once. Both of us had had a few too many beers. Fortunately, my friends had more sense than I did. What about you?"

She laughed. "No. I'm definitely not the fighting type."

"I don't think one bar fight makes your dad a violent man," Ryan said. "And having done time doesn't make him a bad person."

"When they talked about him, it was like they were describing a stranger," she said. "Someone I don't know."

"Our parents are always strangers to us in a way. They lived whole lives before we were ever born, and we can't know that side of them."

"What if they're right and my father did those things?" she asked. "I don't think he knew about the field trip to the mine, but there are workers there. If he set a bomb, it was with the intent to hurt people."

He sighed, and squeezed her shoulder gently. "If your dad did do that, it doesn't make you a bad person. And it doesn't mean you'll stop loving him."

"It will change how I think about him, and maybe how I feel about him," she said.

"It will be hard," he conceded. "But you'll get through it."

"Will I?"

"You won't be alone." He kissed her and held her close. She lay down beside him once more and told herself she was safe here, but she had felt that before and been wrong.

Chapter Eleven

The meeting at search and rescue headquarters Thursday evening was supposed to be about cleaning out the Beast and brainstorming ways to raise money to purchase a new rescue vehicle. But as team members unloaded supplies from the old Jeep, the main topic of conversation was the two strangers who were staying at Hannah Richards's parents' inn. "I think they're some kind of federal agents," Hannah said as she sorted through a plastic tub of supplies from the Beast. "They paid with a government-issued credit card."

"FBI agents," Danny said. He examined a packet of gauze and tossed it into a bin labeled Expired Supplies.

"Alcohol, Tobacco, and Firearm agents," Ryan said. "And Explosives. They're here to investigate the explosion at the Zenith Mine."

Everyone stopped working to stare at him. "How do you know that?" Austen Morrissey asked. He was crouched in the back of the Beast, charged with fishing out anything that had rolled under the seats.

Ryan silently cursed his inability to keep his mouth

FREE BOOKS GIVEAWAY

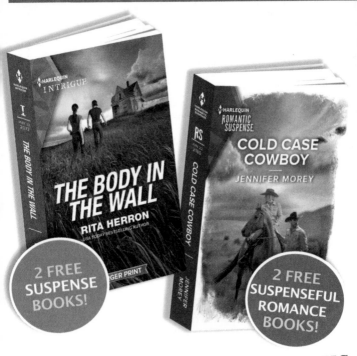

2 FREE SUSPENSE BOOKS!

2 FREE SUSPENSEFUL ROMANCE BOOKS!

GET UP TO FOUR FREE BOOKS & TWO FREE GIFTS WORTH OVER $20!

We pay for everything!

YOU pick your books – WE pay for everything.
You get up to FOUR New Books and TWOMystery Gifts...absolutely FREE!

Dear Reader,

I am writing to announce the launch of a huge **FREE BOOKS GIVEAWAY**... and to let you know that YOU are entitled to choose up to FOUR fantastic books that WE pay for.

Try **Harlequin® Romantic Suspense** books featuring heart-racing page-turners with unexpected plot twists and irresistible chemistry that will keep you guessing to the very end.

Try **Harlequin Intrigue® Larger-Print** books featuring action-packed stories that will keep you on the edge of your seat. Solve the crime and deliver justice at all costs.

Or **TRY BOTH!**

In return, we ask just one favor: Would you please participate in our brief Reader Survey? We'd love to hear from you.

This FREE BOOKS GIVEAWAY means that your introductory shipment is completely free, <u>even the shipping</u>! If you decide to continue, you can look forward to curated monthly shipments of brand-new books from your selected series, always at a discount off the cover price! <u>Plus you can cancel any time</u>. Who could pass up a deal like that?

Sincerely

Pam Powers

Pam Powers
For Harlequin Reader Service

Complete the survey below and return it today to receive up to 4 FREE BOOKS and FREE GIFTS guaranteed!

shut, but he was in too deep to back out now. "They stopped by Deni's Monday night to talk to her."

"Why did they want to talk to Deni?" Sheri asked.

Ryan tried for a bored expression. "I guess because she was in the mine when the explosion happened."

"You guess?" Ted asked. "Don't you know? You were there, weren't you?"

"How do you know I was there?"

Eldon laughed. "We drove by Deni's last night and saw your truck in the driveway."

"It was still there this morning," Ted said.

Ryan flushed. He had mixed feelings about spending the night with Deni. The sex had been great, but how would she feel when she found out her dad wasn't the only one who had done time in prison? Given how upset she was after Agents Olivera and Ferris had badgered her, he hadn't felt right giving her any more distressing news. Now that the feds were involved, he really should take a step back, but he couldn't.

Watching Olivera and Ferris accuse her of helping her father plant bombs had brought back memories of when had had endured similar questions. Except in his case, he really had broken the law. He might not always be a good judge of other people, but he was pretty sure Deni was innocent.

"How is Deni doing?" Sheri asked. "I can't even imagine how horrible it must have been for her."

"She was pretty shaken up, but she'll be okay," Ryan said.

"Did those agents say if the explosion at the mine was caused by a bomb?" Tony asked.

"They asked a lot of questions, but they didn't offer any information," Ryan said.

"Mom says they don't say much of anything," Hannah reported.

"Where's Jake?" Danny asked. "He could probably tell us."

"Jake is working," Hannah said. "And he wouldn't tell you anything. He doesn't talk about his work."

"But does he tell you?" Danny nudged her. "Then you could tell us."

"I have better things to do with Jake than talk about cop stuff," she said, which prompted shouts of laughter from the others.

"I think it had to have been a bomb," Danny said. "What else would cause that kind of destruction?"

The mood of the room immediately sobered. "What kind of nut is planting all these bombs?" Eldon asked. "It's freaky."

"I heard Mike Traynor was a suspect," Austen said. "After all, didn't he go missing about the time they found that first bomb at Grizzly Creek?"

"Is that why the feds wanted to talk to Deni?" Danny asked.

"They didn't say why they were there," Ryan said. "And it doesn't matter, because Deni doesn't know where her dad is or what he's up to."

"I always liked Mike," Ted observed. "He was kind of quiet, but I always thought he was the kind of guy who lived his beliefs."

"What were his beliefs?" Ryan asked.

"Oh, I don't know," Ted said. "But he didn't like development and using up resources, so he lived off-grid on that mining claim. He certainly didn't use a lot of resources. I don't want to live like that, but I can appreciate the integrity of it."

"Didn't Ted Kaczynski live in a cabin in the woods?" Danny asked.

"Who was Ted Kaczynski?" Hannah asked.

"The Unabomber?" Danny asked. "People probably said he was quiet and kept to himself, too."

"This area is full of people who want to live simply and keep to themselves," Sheri said. "That doesn't make them criminals."

"Well, whoever is planting these bombs, I hope they find him soon," Danny said. "I don't like cleaning up after him. It's bad enough all the people who have been injured, but sooner or later someone is going to be killed. Not to mention the ice-climbing area is a mess. It will probably be closed for the rest of the year."

Ryan let the talk swirl around him, his thoughts in turmoil. What if Deni's dad did those things? How could he be related to someone as good as Deni?

"Maybe you should cool things a little with Deni, in case her dad does turn out to be the bomber," Austen said. "You don't want to be tangled up in something like that."

Ryan's first instinct was to be offended, to protest that this didn't involve Deni. Even if her dad was guilty, she hadn't done anything wrong. But when he was really honest with himself, he could admit shying away from the thought of being associated, however peripherally, with someone who had hurt so many people with such destruction. That would be the sensible thing to do, but his past proved he wasn't always sensible, especially when it came to women.

DENI WAS READY when Ryan arrived at her house Friday morning. "If we're going to figure out what's going on with Dad, we need a plan," she told him. She produced a small spiral-bound notebook. "I figure the sheriff's department and maybe the federal cops have been searching for him, but the sheriff's department as much as said he wasn't at the top of their list, and the feds just got here. Plus, it will take them a while to figure out his habits or talk to the people he knew. I feel foolish, not thinking to do this before."

"You're not foolish," he said. "You were upset and afraid. Human."

"I'm still all that," she added. "But I'm also determined to find Dad and figure out what's going on." She leaned toward Ryan. "I know I told the sheriff Dad's been behaving oddly, and that I was worried he might have had something to do with the bombs. But the more I think about it, the more I believe he would never do something that would hurt other people or put them in danger."

Ryan pursed his lips, considering this. "So, if a bomb destroyed a bridge that wasn't open to traffic or kept a company from ever reopening a mine, you think Mike might do that?"

"Exactly." She sighed. "I know that's still horrible, and a criminal act, but I could almost picture him upset enough to do something like that. I don't think he would ever injure or kill a bunch of random people. Not climbers or motorists or mine workers, and certainly not children."

"You already said your father didn't know about the field trip," Ryan pointed out.

"Maybe this conviction that my father is innocent doesn't make sense," she said. "But this was the man who gave money to the hitchhikers he picked up while he was driving—even though that was against company policy. He was always interested in people's stories. He taught me to pick up litter and keep a clean campsite, to take care of the earth. He cared deeply about history and nature—he wanted to preserve places, not destroy them."

Ryan listened, not interrupting or contradicting her. "Okay," he said when she finally fell silent. "So what's the plan?"

Some of the tension in her chest eased. If Ryan did think she was wrong about her dad, he at least was still willing to come with her to try and find him. She opened her notebook. "First stop, Rouster's Coffee Roasters."

"Your dad liked Rouster's coffee?"

"He liked Rouster—Rusty Wilson."

"Then let's go."

Rusty "Rouster" Wilson roasted his coffee in a barn-like building in an industrial park on the far edge of Eagle Mountain, a block from the waste transfer station and across the highway from the sewage treatment facility. "Dad came here two or three mornings a week to have coffee with Rouster," Deni said as Ryan pulled his truck into a lot that contained a stack of old pallets and a mud-spattered FJ with green primer on the front right quarter panel.

"I thought the place only sold wholesale coffee beans," Ryan said after they had climbed out of the truck.

"It does. Rouster's Roast is served at restaurants all over Colorado and half of Utah." She walked to the front door and rang the bell. "But Dad didn't know that the first time he came here. He saw the sign that said Coffee and pulled in to buy a cup. Rouster tried to direct him to one of the cafés in town, but Dad wouldn't take no for an answer. Finally, Rouster invited him in and brewed up a fresh pot."

"The next morning he showed up again, this time with muffins from the bakery," a deep voice said. The door opened and a stocky man with a full red beard greeted them. "Where is the old cuss, Deni?" he asked. "I'm almost starting to miss him."

"Hi, Rouster," Deni said. "This is my friend Ryan."

The two men shook hands. "We want to talk to you about Dad," Deni said.

"Come on in." He opened the door wider and led the way down a short hall, into a room redolent with the aroma of roasting coffee. The space was dominated by a gleaming stainless steel and blue enamel roaster that looked to Deni like a cross between a robot and a giant washing machine. The machine roared softly, radiating heat and the heady scent of roasting coffee. Burlap bags of coffee beans stamped with their country of origin were stacked thigh-high along one wall.

"Have a seat." Rouster motioned to a sagging green sofa, and walked to a silver coffee urn on a nearby counter. "I haven't heard a word out of Mike in over two weeks," Rouster said as he measured ground coffee into the machine. "Have you?"

"No." She sank onto the sofa, which sagged so low her knees were at midchest. She moved to the edge of the seat and sat up straighter. "I'm trying to put together a picture of what he was up to before he disappeared," she said. "When was the last time you saw him?"

Rouster pulled three mugs from a cabinet above the coffee maker. "Monday, March 8. I know because that's my birthday and instead of muffins, Mike brought cupcakes." His voice roughened on the last words and he cleared his throat. "The old cuss never said anything about leaving town."

The coffee maker began to hiss and spit. "Cream and sugar?" Rouster asked.

"Both," she said.

"Black for me," Ryan said.

"Mike drank his coffee black, too," Rouster said. He stared at the coffee maker, his expression glum.

"Did Dad say anything about wanting to change things around here?" Deni asked.

"What do you mean?" Rouster tore his gaze away from the coffee.

"Well, you know he wasn't a big fan of the Zenith Mine reopening."

"Mike didn't like change of any kind." He filled the first mug, steam rising in a cloud around him. "I told him all the time he was too young to be so set in his ways."

"But did he ever say anything about doing anything to stop change from happening?" she asked.

He handed her the mug, along with a ceramic bowl of sugar and creamer packets. "He went to a lot of meetings and protests. He wrote letters. That kind of thing."

"Did he ever talk about bombs?" Ryan's words were an explosion of their own, shattering the calm in the room.

"He never said anything like that." Rouster glared at Deni. "Is that what you think? That Mike is the one who's been blowing up stuff around here?"

"No! Of course not!" She spread her hands wide. "But he's gone, and everyone knows he didn't like the places the bombs have targeted. And he knew about explosives from the military…" Saying all that out loud sounded so bad, but that didn't make her father a bomber.

Rouster shook his head. "I can't believe it. And I'm telling you the truth when I say he never talked about anything like that. We spent hours right there on that couch, talking about everything under the sun. He complained plenty, but he never, ever suggested violence."

"He never said anything like that to me, either," she said. "But I figured he might be different with his friends than he was with me."

"He never advocated violence around me," Rouster said. He took a long drink of coffee, frown lines deep across his forehead. "He was a little 'off' last time I saw him."

"In what way?" Ryan asked.

"Hard to say. Distracted. I asked him what was wrong and he blew me off, said something like 'nothing important' and changed the subject."

"And he never said anything about wanting to get away for a while?" Ryan asked. "Maybe take a trip, go to see old friends, anything like that?"

"No, and if he was going to do something like that, he would have told Deni." He turned to her. "Your daddy loves you and he is so proud of you. He said moving here to be close to you was one of the best things he ever did."

She opened her eyes wide, trying to blink past the tears, and swallowed the lump in her throat. Ryan sent her a sympathetic look, then, perhaps to give her a moment to compose herself, asked, "Can you think of anyone else we should talk to? Any other friends he hung out with?"

"Mike was pretty much a loner." Rouster set down his cup and walked over to the coffee roaster and studied the dial. He made some adjustments, then returned to them. "There was one guy, Al somebody. Mike brought him here one morning, but I told him not to bring him back."

"Why is that?"

"I didn't like him," Rouster said. "He used a lot of foul language and was talking trash about pretty much everybody. Mike would complain about people, but he was upset about the things they did. Al referred to one of the city council members as a communist and said some really nasty stuff I won't repeat about one of the women on the council. I don't want anything to do with someone like that and I told Mike so."

"I never heard Dad mention anyone like that," Deni said. "Did Dad say how they knew each other?"

"I think they met when a bunch of people went up to the Zenith Mine to protest," Rouster said. "Mike introduced him as 'somebody who thinks a lot like I do,' but he was wrong. Your dad has never been mean. This guy was."

"Al what?" Ryan asked. "Do you know his last name?"

Rouster shook his head. "I don't think I ever knew."

"Can you remember anything else about him?" Ryan asked. "Where he worked, or where he lived?"

"Mike and him talked like he lived in a cabin off-grid, like Mike. He might even have said they were neighbors." Rouster shook his head. "Sorry I don't remember more. I didn't like the guy, so I didn't want to know anything else about him. But if you can find him, maybe he knows what's up with your dad."

They thanked him for the coffee and information and left. "What now?" Ryan asked.

"I'm trying to think of someone who might know more about Al," she said.

"Your dad never mentioned him?"

"No. And that's a little odd. I mean, I guess I don't know everything about Dad, but when we talked, he often told me what he'd been up to that day, who he had seen, etc. I'm sure he never mentioned anyone named Al. He really never mentioned any friends, except Rouster." She tried to remember conversations with her father, in particular ones where he mentioned names of people he had talked to. She fastened her seat belt. "Do you know where Broken Spur Antiques is?"

"Is that one of the shops on the square?"

"That's the one. A woman named Glenda owns it. She knew Dad. Let's see what she has to say."

Ryan put the truck in gear and headed toward downtown. "How does your dad know Glenda? Were they just friends, or did they date?"

She laughed. "Nothing that close. She organizes a lot of the protests around here and is always lobbying the city council for different environmental and political causes. She got them to set up a recycling program at the transfer station and I'm pretty sure she was one of the leaders of the protest at the Zenith Mine."

Glenda Nassib looked up from behind a desk when Deni and Ryan entered her small antique shop. "May I help you?" she asked, in an accent that carried a hint of the East Coast.

"I'm Deni Traynor. Mike Traynor's daughter."

Glenda stood. "I saw the posters about Mike going missing," she said. "I was so sorry to hear that."

"This is Ryan Welch," Deni said. "We're trying to put together a timeline of what Dad was doing right before he disappeared. I was wondering when you saw him last."

Glenda shook her head. "I haven't seen Mike in a long time. Weeks."

"You helped organize the protest up at the Zenith Mine, didn't you?" Deni asked.

"Yes. And that may have been the last time I saw

him. Or, no—the last time was at one of the meetings to oppose the proposed expansion of the Nugget Hotel."

"How did he seem to you then?" Ryan asked.

Glenda shrugged. "The same. He was frustrated that nothing we were doing seemed to be working. We protested, we wrote letters, we voiced our concerns, but it was as if nobody was listening."

"That sounds pretty frustrating," Ryan said.

"It can be, but I try to tell people, it's part of the process. I've been at this a long time, and you learn that there are always more failures than victories, but it's still worth it to make a dissenting view heard, and over time, you can change the way people think. Just the other day over in Lake County, a developer we've argued with for years presented a proposal for a new housing development. Only this time, he included several of the things we've been advocating for over the years—green space, trails, water-wise landscaping. It's progress." She smiled. "But I understand, people get upset when things take so long to change."

"Was Mike upset about the mine?" Ryan asked.

"He was, but not unusually so." She turned to Deni. "Your father is passionate about his desire to maintain the quality of life and natural beauty we all enjoy here. You should be proud of that."

"I am," Deni said. But pride was a poor substitute for having her dad back home. "Do you know anything about a man named Al? Rouster Wilson told us he and Dad were friends, and that they met at the Zenith Mine protest."

"That name isn't familiar to me." She tilted her head.

"There was a man named Alex. He was maybe five foot six inches, with a heavy dark beard and horn-rimmed glasses. Could that be him?"

Deni realized they hadn't bothered to ask Rouster what Al looked like. They would have to go back and ask. "I don't know. Do you know his last name?"

"If I did, I've forgotten it," Glenda said. "I really only saw him a couple of times—at the mine, and at that council meeting about the hotel expansion. Come to think of it, he and your dad were there together, it seems. Or at least, they were sitting next to each other."

"What was Alex like?" Ryan asked.

She frowned. "Belligerent. Not a good listener. He interrupted people and had a foul mouth. He said we were wasting our time if we expected anyone to change their minds if money was involved."

"What did he think you should do instead?" Ryan wanted to know.

"He didn't say," Glenda said.

"Do you know where he lived, or if he had a job?" Ryan asked.

"I don't. And like I said, I haven't seen him in a long time, either. Probably since that council meeting."

The sleigh bells attached to the back of the door jangled as two women entered. "I'll let you get back to work," Deni said. "Thanks."

"I hope you find your father," Glenda said. "He can be a bit of curmudgeon, but his heart is in the right place."

They left the store. "We need to ask Rouster what Al looked like," Deni said.

"It's interesting that neither Glenda nor Rouster—if Al and Alex are the same person—have seen him since your dad disappeared," Ryan said. "Do you think they could have left together?"

"I have no idea what to think," Deni admitted.

A sign on the door informed them that Rouster was away for the rest of the day. "What do we do now?" Ryan asked.

"Rouster said he thought Dad and Al might be neighbors," Deni said. "There aren't that many places to live near my dad. It's mostly unoccupied mining claims. Let's see if we can find a neighbor to talk to."

"Al doesn't sound like a very pleasant person," Ryan said.

"No." She leaned over and patted his arm. "That's why I have you along."

"To protect you?"

She grinned. "I figure if things get ugly, you can distract them while I run away."

He attempted to look offended, but ended up laughing with her. It was a good sign, still finding something to laugh about in spite of all the sadness around her.

Chapter Twelve

Ryan headed his truck toward Mike Traynor's cabin, but slowed near the turnoff. "Someone else has been up this way recently," he said, pointing ahead to the tracks in the snow. "Maybe they were headed to another cabin? Maybe we should follow them."

"OK." Deni leaned forward in her seat. "The road doesn't look too bad—like someone cleared it recently."

"That's a good indicator someone is living up this way." Ryan started forward again, moving slowly and trying to stay in the tracks of the person who had gone before them. Though the road had been plowed sometime since the last big storm, the snow was probably soft on the edges and he didn't want to get stuck.

They had traveled about a quarter mile when he caught a flash of pink by the side of the road. "That surveyor's tape looks pretty new," Deni said.

As they drew nearer, they could see the tape was marking the entry into a driveway. Sure enough, the tracks they had been following turned in there. Ryan followed them, hoping he wasn't getting into someplace he couldn't get out of easily.

Unlike Mike Traynor's place, which could be reached only by snowmobile or on foot in winter, this drive was cleared all the way to the dwelling at the end of it— not a cabin, but a yurt, with green canvas sides, smoke puffing from a black pipe protruding from the roof.

Ryan hadn't even shut off the engine of the truck when a man appeared in the door of the yurt. He was stocky, of average height, clean-shaven, with a black watch cap pulled down over his ears. He watched as Ryan and Deni got out of the truck and walked toward him. "Hello," Deni called. "This is a beautiful place you've got here. Do you like living in a yurt?"

"What can I do for you?" The man wasn't unfriendly, but he seemed wary. Or maybe shy.

"I'm Mike Traynor's daughter, Deni." Deni offered a warm smile. "I don't know if you've met my dad, but he's probably your closest neighbor." She gestured in the direction of Mike's cabin. "I was wondering if you've seen him recently."

"I guess I've seen him around, but I don't know him," the man said. "But I pretty much keep to myself."

"When was the last time you saw my dad?" Deni asked.

"Couldn't say."

"What's your name?" Ryan asked. "I'm Ryan, by the way."

The man's expression remained impassive. "My name's not important," he said.

Ryan was taken aback. How could he counter that?

"Dad's been missing a couple of weeks," Deni said. "I'm really worried about him."

"Sorry, I can't help you." The man turned and went back inside, the door closing softly behind him.

Deni and Ryan looked at each other. "I guess we'd better go," he said.

Neither of them said anything until they were in the truck and out of the driveway. "He certainly wasn't very friendly," Deni said.

"He didn't look like Glenda described Alex," Ryan said.

"We still need to talk to Rouster again about Al." She leaned her head back and closed her eyes. "Let's stop by Dad's on the way out." She didn't say "just in case he's been there" but Ryan thought that was what she meant.

"No problem," he said, and headed back the way they had come.

He parked at the cleared-out space and they hiked up to the house. The path was well packed by now, so they didn't need snowshoes. "Someone else has been here," Deni said, pointing to the packed trail.

"Probably the cops," Ryan said. "They said they would look for your dad, and his house is the best place to start."

"Then why didn't they tell me what they found?" she asked.

He shrugged. She didn't want to hear that law enforcement didn't readily share information with family, especially if the person they were investigating was suspected of a crime.

The ladder still sat under the window, and the same

few items lay undisturbed on the workbench. Deni's shoulders slumped. "It doesn't look like Dad is here."

Ryan put his arm around her. "You've done a lot today."

She turned away. "I guess it was foolish to think we could actually find Dad today," she said. "When all the cops looking for him haven't been able to track him down."

"We haven't come up completely dry," Ryan said. "We learned about Al."

"Who also, apparently, has disappeared."

They started back down the path toward the truck. "Maybe Al and your dad ran off together," Ryan said.

She frowned. "I can't really see that, but who knows?" She sighed. "Let's go home."

Back in the truck, he drove down the mountain on the narrow snow-packed forest service road. They were traveling at about twenty-five miles an hour when a roaring sound filled the cab. Ryan looked up to see a large black truck gaining on them. Deni turned to look back. "What is that guy doing, driving that fast on this road?" she asked.

"I don't know, but he's not slowing down." He pumped his brakes and edged over to the side. There was plenty of room to pass if the guy was careful.

But the driver of the black pickup didn't slow down, and he didn't move over. "What the h—?" Ryan didn't get to finish the sentence. The truck driver laid on the horn and the engine revved even louder. Ryan wrenched the steering wheel to the right and felt the tires slip off the road and sink into the soft snow. He wrestled the steering wheel, trying to steer back onto the solid surface, but it was too late, the black truck rocketed past as Ryan's truck tipped, then began to roll.

DENI SCREAMED AS she was thrown against the seat belts. The truck air bag exploded, hard against her forearms, filling the air with a cloud of white. Her head banged against the side of the truck, then the back, and her chest constricted with terror. "Ryan!" she called.

He didn't answer, though she could see him strapped in beside her, his fingers gripping the steering wheel as if he could somehow still control the vehicle.

With a painful jolt, they came to a halt. She was tilted sharply to the right, her body angled down, the seat belt holding her in place, her head pounding. She gripped the side of her seat, heart hammering wildly, and tried to see out, but the window was splintered by dozens of cracks.

"Ryan!" she called again, and looked over at him. He, too, was suspended by his seat belt, his body limp, blood flowing from a gash on his head. "Ryan!" she shouted, louder this time. She tried to reach out and touch him, but couldn't quite close the gap.

Surely the driver of that black truck would see what had happened and would stop to help. She listened for approaching footsteps, but could hear nothing but the ping of the truck engine as it cooled and the creak of the vehicle settling against whatever had stopped its fall. "Help!" she shouted. "Somebody help!"

Ryan moaned, and she turned her attention to him once more. "Ryan! Wake up. Please wake up."

He moaned again, and struggled against the seat belt. "Talk to me," she said. "Tell me you're okay."

His eyelids fluttered, and he groaned louder. At last his eyes opened and he turned his head to look at her. "Are you okay?" he asked.

"I'm fine," she said, her voice shaky with relief. "But you're bleeding."

He touched a hand to the blood on his head and winced. "It's okay," he answered. "Head wounds always bleed a lot."

"That guy didn't even stop to help," she said. "Do you think he ran us off the road on purpose?"

"Maybe. Did you get a good look at him?" Ryan asked.

"No. His windows were tinted, I think. And everything happened so fast."

He fumbled with his seat belt, but it refused to release. "How are we going to get out of here?" she asked. "There's no phone signal here."

"Can you reach the glove box and open it?"

She braced herself against the door and reached out. She had to punch the release button three times, but at last the door to the glove box popped open. "What am I looking for?"

"There's a tool in there with an orange handle."

She spotted bright orange and pulled out a heavy bar and handed it to him. He popped a catch on it and a wicked-looking curved blade was exposed. "Let me cut myself free and I'll help you," he said, and began sawing at the seat belt.

Sweat was beading on his forehead and he was

breathing hard by the time he had managed to cut through the belt. Then he had to brace against the steering wheel and turn upright. He leaned across the center console and began sawing at Deni's seat belt. "You're the only person I know who carries something like this in your vehicle," she said.

"I've worked enough rescues where people were trapped in their cars to know I didn't want to be in that situation. One guy hung upside down for six hours before we got to him."

She grimaced. Even though they weren't completely upside down, the position she was in was uncomfortable. Before too much longer, it would probably be painful.

The strap broke and she sagged down, and banged her arm against the door. Still clutching the tool, Ryan crawled back across the console and attacked the driver's side door. At first it refused to budge, but when he threw his body against it, it finally opened, with a wrenching sound that would have been suitable for a horror film. He crawled up and out, then leaned back in to offer a hand to Deni. "We're up against a big tree," he said. "There are a lot of branches and stuff you'll have to fight through."

"I don't care. I want out of this truck." She pulled herself toward the door and he helped her climb out. Then they had to jump to the ground, sinking into the snow, a juniper branch slapping her in the face.

Carefully, they made their way around the truck, holding on to the frame and each other for balance. When they emerged onto the roadway she leaned against him.

"Are you sure you're okay?" he asked. "Did you hit your head?"

"I'm fine." She put a hand to your head. "I did bang my head, but it doesn't even hurt."

"Let me see." He ran her hands through her hair, his gentle touch sending a tremor through her. "There's no blood and I can't feel a bump." He looked into her eyes. "Your pupils look okay. How about the rest of you?"

"A few bruises, but that's all." She looked up at him, the sight of all that blood still alarming. "But you look like you're hurt."

"I hit my head pretty hard. I might need stitches. I might even have a concussion. But there's no way to know until we get to someplace where I can be checked out." He pulled out his phone and frowned. "No signal here to call for help."

"Dad has a cell booster," she said. "We can call from there. He probably has a first-aid kit, too."

"Good idea." They were only a few hundred yards from the turnoff to her dad's cabin, but after that they had another quarter mile to walk. By the time they arrived at their destination, she was chilled through. Beside her, she could feel Ryan shaking. "We need to get inside and get a fire going," she said.

The padlock they had seen on the door on their earlier visit was gone, replaced by a lockbox and an official seal Property of Rayford County Sheriff's Department. They stared at the lock. "That doesn't look good," Ryan said.

Deni shook her head. "We have to get in." She headed

for the ladder. "I'll go in the window and come down and unlock the back door. There's a dead bolt on it, but I can open it from the inside."

Ryan looked as if he wanted to object, then nodded and leaned against the porch, his face gray. She prayed he wasn't going to pass out while she was trying to get them in.

She struggled several minutes to force open the window, but at last she was able to raise the sash enough to allow her to climb in. She didn't hesitate, but raced down the stairs from the loft to the ground floor, and to the back door, where she turned all the locks and threw the door open. "Ryan!" she called.

He appeared around the side of the house. At the door, she took his hands and tugged him inside, over to a chair at the table. "Sit here while I start the fire, then we'll see about getting you cleaned up, and we'll call someone to come get us."

He didn't protest that he could help, which told her again how bad he must be feeling. She found split wood and kindling in an old copper wash boiler beside the woodstove, and set about making a fire. Within minutes, a blaze was licking at the wood. It would take a while longer for the cabin to warm, but the fire itself lifted her spirits.

Next, she filled a kettle at the sink, the small electric pump that drew from the reservoir tank outside the cabin humming reassuringly as the slightly rusty water flowed. She lit a burner on the propane stove and set the kettle to heat. "When that is boiling, I'll pour some off to clean up some of that blood."

"A mirror would help me get a better look at it," he said.

"I think there's one in the bedroom. I'll get it in a minute."

He closed his eyes, then opened them again. "I can still see that truck barreling down on us, but I can't picture the driver, or a license plate. I can't even tell you what make of truck it was. It was so unexpected."

"It was terrifying." She dropped into the chair across from him and studied his face. Blood smeared one cheek and matted his hair, but his eyes were focused and clear. "How are you feeling?" she asked.

"I have a headache. I think I hit it against the window." He touched the wound again. "I should be okay. We're lucky that tree was there to stop our fall. But my truck is a wreck."

The kettle began to hiss, so she stood, poured some of the water into a bowl to cool, and went in search of some clean rags and a mirror. She found what she wanted, as well as a first-aid kit with gauze pads and some antibiotic ointment. "This probably isn't going to feel so great, but we need to clean up that blood and get a look at the wound," she said.

He didn't say anything beyond letting out a low hiss at one point when she dabbed at the jagged wound just above his temple. The gash was about two inches long, but not too deep. Once she had cleaned off most of the blood, she handed him the mirror. "Take a look."

He studied his reflection. "Put some of that antibiotic ointment on it, and a gauze pad and I'll be good," he said. "I think I can even get away without stitches."

She did as he asked, then glanced out the window at the fading light. "I'd better call. Do you have a friend who would come get us?"

"Call the sheriff," Ryan said. "We need to report that guy who ran us off the road."

She wanted to protest, but knew he was right. She pulled out the phone and stared at the screen. "It says No Service," she noted. "That can't be right."

She looked around for the cell booster and antennae that usually sat on a shelf above her father's recliner. But the shelf was empty. She drew nearer, but saw no sign of the equipment. "There was a cell booster right here," she said.

"Maybe your dad moved it."

But a quick search of the house revealed no booster. And she couldn't raise a signal no matter where she stood. "I think we should spend the night here and hike out to the road in the morning," she observed. "I'm not comfortable going back to the yurt to ask for help, and it's too late to start walking now. We'll be warm and safe here, and there's food and a place to sleep."

"I was going to suggest the same thing," he said. He looked toward the kitchen. "What does your dad have in the way of food? I'm starving."

"Dad is no gourmet," she said. "But he'll have something."

"Something" proved to be canned chili and boxed macaroni and cheese, but the chili-mac concoction she made was delicious. They ate it all, and were clearing away the dishes when a bright light suddenly shone through the front window, and a voice boomed: "This is the police. Come out with your hands up!"

Chapter Thirteen

Ryan froze, squinting in the bright light that seemed focused right in his eyes. "What is going on?" Deni asked. She stood at his elbow, a water glass in each hand, while he carried a stack of plates and silverware.

"I don't know," he said, as the voice boomed again that they needed to come out.

He set the dishes back on the table. "We'd better do as they say."

She set aside the glasses and followed him to the door. "We're coming out!" he shouted.

"Please don't shoot," Deni said, though not loud enough for anyone outside to hear.

Ryan eased open the door and together they stepped outside, hands in the air. At first he didn't see anyone, then Travis stepped out from behind the woodpile. "You can put your hands down," he said, and holstered his weapon. "We saw the lights and the smoke and didn't know who was in there."

"What are you doing here?" Deni asked.

"We came up to search the place again." He looked behind her to the open door. "What are you doing here?"

"We were driving around, looking for Dad," she said. "Someone ran us off the road. This was the closest place we could come."

Travis walked over to him. Two other deputies emerged from hiding and stood a few feet away. "Looks like you got a little banged up," he said, taking in Ryan's bandaged head. He looked to Deni. "Are you okay?"

"A few bruises, but I'm all right." She hugged her arms around her shoulders, cold without a coat. "The truck is up the road, off the side, up against a tree."

"Let's go inside where it's warmer." Travis nodded toward the door. "I'll send Jake and Dwight to look at the truck."

Deni and Ryan returned to the cabin. A few moments later, the sheriff entered. "Who ran you off the road?" he asked.

"Someone in a black pickup with tinted windows," Ryan said. "They came up behind us, blaring the horn. When I tried to move over to let them pass, my tires slipped into the soft snow on the edge and we rolled."

"We had just been to talk to the guy in the yurt up the road," she said. "We asked him about Dad, but he said he didn't know anything."

Travis frowned. "I know the yurt you're talking about, but I thought it was a summer home. What's the guy's name?"

"He refused to tell us," Ryan said. "He wasn't very friendly. I even wondered if he was the one in the truck."

"Did you get a license plate number?" Travis asked.

Ryan shook his head. "It all happened so fast," Deni said. "It was terrifying."

Ryan took her hand and squeezed it. Her fingers were ice-cold.

"We'll check him out and take a look at his vehicle," Travis said. He looked around the cabin. "Did you find anything to tell you where your dad might be?"

"We haven't even looked," she said. "But we talked to a couple of people in town who know Dad. They mentioned that he had been hanging out with a new friend named Al or Alex. Rouster Wilson said he was foul-mouthed and negative, and Glenda Nassib described him as belligerent."

"Your dad never mentioned this man to you?" Travis asked.

"No. And it doesn't sound like someone he would want to be around." She shrugged. "Rouster said he thought Al and my dad were neighbors, but Glenda described Alex as having a black beard and horn-rimmed glasses. The man we met at the yurt was clean-shaven and didn't wear glasses."

"It's easy enough to shave and take off a pair of glasses," Travis said. He looked around the room again. "We'd like to come in and look around, but I can have Jake drive you back to town. We'll call for a wrecker to retrieve your truck. Is it okay to take it to O'Brien's garage?"

"That would be great," Ryan said. He didn't even want to think about how much the bill to repair the vehicle would be—if it wasn't a total loss.

While they waited for the deputies to return, Ryan

and Deni washed dishes and banked the fire. A knock announced Dwight and Jake's arrival. Travis opened the door for the men and they came in, stamping their feet and rubbing their hands together. "We found the truck," Dwight said. "About a quarter mile up the road. No skid marks. Looks like whoever came up on you didn't even slow down."

"Jake, I'd like you to take Deni and Ryan back to town. Dwight and I are going to question a guy who lives in a yurt down the road. You can meet us back up here to search this place when you're done."

"Do you mean Ed Brubaker's yurt?" Dwight asked.

"You know him?" Deni asked.

"He and his family come for a couple of months every summer and stay in that yurt," Dwight said. "Ed's a big fly fisherman and his wife paints."

"What does he look like?" Ryan asked.

"Tall and skinny. Little gray beard. He's in his seventies now, but he still come up to fish every year. Sometimes one of his boys uses the place, but I've never met them."

"Maybe one of them is in the yurt now," Travis said. "We'll drive down there and see while Jake takes Deni and Ryan home."

Ryan asked Jake to stop by the truck so he could retrieve his pack. He could hardly bear to look too closely at the damage, but what he saw was enough to make his heart sink. He and Deni were lucky they hadn't been hurt worse.

As soon as they were headed out in the sheriff's department SUV, Jake said, "What happened with the guy in the yurt?"

Ryan explained about their visit, and being run off the road by the black pickup shortly afterward. "I've never met Ed Brubaker or his kids, so I can't tell you anything about them," Jake said. "But what reason would one of them have for running you off the road?"

"What reason would anyone have?" Deni asked.

Ryan leaned forward in the seat. "While we've got you here, what do you know about a couple of Alcohol, Tobacco, Firearms and Explosives agents who are in town?"

Jake made a face. "So you've heard about them?"

"They came to my house and started questioning me Monday evening," Deni said. "They were really rude. They all but accused me of helping my dad plant those bombs."

"Some cops find intimidation an effective interrogation technique," Jake said.

"Well, they're not going to get any information out of me, because I don't know anything." Deni hugged her arms across her chest. "Do they really think Dad is involved in all this, or do they treat everyone that way?"

"You said yourself your dad had been acting strange, and you were worried he might be involved," Jake said.

"Yes, but that was before I really thought about it," she said. "Dad complained a lot about development and changes around here, but he would never hurt people. I'm sure of it."

"Have you heard anything about a man named Al or Alex?" Ryan asked. "He supposedly was involved in some of the protests against the hotel expansion and the mine reopening. We talked to a couple of people who said he and Mike were friends."

"I haven't heard anything about him," Jake said. "And as far as what the feds think—they don't let us locals in on that information. They're here because of the bombs at the mine and in Caspar Canyon. That kind of thing is over the head of a small-town department like ours."

"So you aren't investigating the bombings anymore?" Ryan asked.

"We are assisting the feds with their enquiries," Jake said. "And looking for your dad. Not as a suspect," he added. "But as a missing person." He paused, the silence weighted.

"What aren't you telling me?" Deni asked. She scooted as far forward in the back seat as the seat belt would allow. "There's something, isn't there? What have you found out?"

"We checked your dad's accounts at the local bank," Jake said. "That's standard with a missing adult. We can sometimes track people through their credit or debit card activity. But in your dad's case, there hasn't been any."

"You mean, he hasn't used his credit or debit cards?" Deni asked.

"No. That doesn't mean he isn't just paying for everything in cash. People know about being tracked through their cards now, so someone who is trying to hide will often pay for everything in cash."

"But why would Dad be hiding?" Deni asked. Ryan heard the desperation in her voice. "Especially from me?"

"We're not giving up on finding him," Jake said.

"That's why we went up to his cabin today. We're hoping we find something that will give us a clue as to why he left and where he might be."

"His truck, his snowmobile and the trunk where he kept his guns are all missing, right?" Ryan asked her. "Did you notice anything else?"

"No," she said. "But I never went through the closets and everything. Even if I did, I'm not sure I would know what was supposed to be there and what wasn't. He's a private person and I respect that." She shifted. "I mean, do you want to know your father's personal business?"

"No," he said. He couldn't imagine even having a conversation of a personal nature with his father. They didn't have that kind of relationship.

"Just know that we're going to keep looking for him," Jake said. They were nearing town now. "Where should I drop you off?"

"My house," she answered, and gave him the address. "I can take Ryan to his place later." She turned to Ryan. "Or do you want to go to the medical clinic?"

"I'll be fine," he said. "It looked a lot worse than it really was."

Jake had just turned onto Deni's street when his phone rang. He answered and the sheriff asked, "What's your twenty?"

"I'm with Deni and Ryan, just about to drop her off at her house."

"We stopped by the yurt. Someone has been there— we could see tracks where a vehicle, maybe a truck, was parked in back. But there's no one there now. The lock on the door is broken, though."

"Did whoever was there just go to town to run an errand or are they gone for good?" Ryan asked.

"We're going to get in touch with Ed Brubaker and find out," Travis said. "Can you tell us anything more about the truck?"

"Just that it was black and a full-size model." He frowned. "A Chevy or a Ford. A Ram has a different grille, I think."

"And there was no contact between your vehicle and the truck?" Travis asked.

"No, sir. He never hit me—I moved over to try to avoid being hit, and that's when my truck rolled."

"So there's no damage to the other vehicle that we can try to match," Travis said. "Let me know if you remember anything else. In the meantime, keep an eye out for the guy you saw at the yurt. I want to know if you spot him again."

"I will," Ryan said.

Jake pulled into Deni's driveway. "Are you two going to be all right?" he asked.

"We'll be okay," Deni said. "Thanks for the ride."

They got out of the SUV and walked in silence to Deni's door. But once inside, she moved into his arms. "I'm scared," she told him.

He pulled her close. He was afraid for her, but he didn't think saying that would bring her any comfort. "We're going to get through this," he said. "Together."

Chapter Fourteen

Ryan had settled down to watch TV with Deni when the text came in from SAR Captain Tony Meisner. Car off highway at Ruby Falls. "I have to go," he said, standing, the familiar adrenaline rush already firing.

"Are you sure?" she asked. "Your head—"

"It's okay." He touched the bandage. He didn't have any sign of concussion. "I'll be fine. But will you be okay?"

"Of course. What's going on?"

"A car off the road." He started putting on his shoes, then stopped. "I'll have to call someone to give me a ride." That was one aspect of not having his own vehicle that he hadn't thought about.

"Take my car." She got up and fished her keys from her purse. "I'm not going to need it until Monday, really."

"Thanks." He grabbed his jacket and his pack. After a moment's thought, he fished a knitted beanie from the pack and pulled it down low, covering his bandaged head. He didn't feel like answering questions about it right now. Then he headed out toward Ruby Falls.

The scene that greeted the rescuers on their arrival stunned them into momentary silence. The SUV sat upright against the far shore of the icy river, the top partially smashed in, broken glass and pieces of trim scattered among the rocks like party confetti. Some fifty feet from the vehicle two children clung to each other on a boulder, surrounded by icy water. At the sight of the rescuers they began screaming, the terror behind their cries heart-wrenching.

"Don't move!" Tony shouted to them. "Stay right where you are. We'll come to you."

"Mama!" the taller of the two, a girl Ryan thought couldn't be more than six, her long brown hair matted to her head by water or blood or both, gestured toward the SUV. "Mama!"

"We'll take care of your mother," Tony called. "Stay right where you are."

It was easy to see why he kept repeating the admonition—unlike the calmer water where the SUV had landed, the current swept past the boulder on both sides, the water swift and deep enough that it hadn't frozen in this spot. If the children tried to step into that they would be dragged away, to be drowned or frozen within minutes.

"Who's completed swift water rescue training?" Tony searched the group of volunteers who had gathered on the roadside above the place where the car had gone over.

"I have," Ryan said.

"Me, too." Ted stepped forward.

"I've done the training," Eldon said.

Tony eyed Ryan skeptically. "Is your arm up to this?" he asked.

"Yes, sir," Ryan said. Maybe he wasn't up to his preinjury strength yet, but enough time had passed for the soft tissue injury to heal, and those children needed him.

Tony shook his head. "Don't think I don't see that bandage on your head. I heard about what happened up by Mike Traynor's place yesterday. Were you planning to tell me?"

Ryan flushed. "It's not a serious injury," he protested.

"You stay with the crew on shore," Tony said. "I don't think you're up to swift water rescue yet."

"Yes, sir." Ryan knew he had messed up, not telling Tony right away about his head injury, even if he didn't believe it would interfere with his rescue work. All his training had drilled into him that search and rescue wasn't about individual glory, but what was best for the team.

Tony sent Cassie and Jake to see to the mother. "Eldon, you and Ted are with me and Sheri," he said.

Ryan pitched in to assemble the equipment Tony and his group would need. Deputies Jake Gwynn and Jamie Douglas arrived to direct traffic and assist.

The team was setting safety lines when Cassie radioed that the mother had sustained a head injury, was coming in and out of consciousness and was trapped in the partially crushed vehicle. They were going to cut her free with the Jaws of Life. "Then we're going to need Life Flight to get her to the hospital in Junction."

"I'll radio for the chopper." Jamie's voice broke in. "And I've called for a victim's advocate to come be with the children, though if you can find out the name of a local relative who could look after them, that would be even better."

"Thanks," Tony said. "We'll let you know."

The air by the river was even colder than up at the road, the roar of rushing water making it necessary to shout to be heard. The children had stopped crying and crouched on the boulder, the older one's arms wrapped around her younger sibling. Even from his spot on the riverbank, Ryan could see them shivering. The team carried warming packs in their gear, and Sheri had blankets, but would that be enough?

"We're going to cross one at a time," Tony instructed the trio gathered around him. "You'll be clipped in, so if you slip, don't panic. But try not to slip. We don't want to have to treat any of you for hypothermia along with the kids. Eldon, you go first."

Ryan stood by, imagining the shock of the cold water. Eldon grimaced as he waded in, but kept moving. Ryan remembered his training, how the icy liquid seeped through his layers of clothing. Within two steps he could no longer feel his feet. Two more steps and his skin was on fire.

Eldon gripped the safety line, clenched his jaw and kept moving forward, his focus on the kids. Halfway to them, he slipped on an icy rock and landed on his back in the water. The current pulled at him as he struggled to regain his footing. Ryan leaned forward, his body tensed, fighting rising panic as he watched his friend struggle. He hated being stuck here, unable to help. Maybe he wasn't as strong as he should be, but he ought to be able to do something.

The older child let go of her sibling and leaned out from the rock. "No!" Ryan shouted. "Stay there and someone will come to you!"

Eldon managed to crawl out of the water on hands and knees. His teeth chattered and he struggled to open his pack. There was scarcely enough room on the boulder for the two kids, so he was forced to remain half in the water. "Don't send anyone else," he radioed back. "There's nowhere to put them."

He spoke to the children, then wrapped them each in foil emergency blankets from his pack. He radioed back that the children's names were Tamsin and Owen. Tamsin helped wrap her little brother in his blanket, then Eldon tucked warming packs inside their wet clothing.

"Tamsin said she bumped her head, but there's no open wound," Eldon radioed. "They're both very cold and shivering, but no obvious injuries. I want to get them out of here to where they can get warm as soon as possible."

"Bring the smallest child back with you and I'll send Sheri over for the older one," Tony radioed.

"Copy that," Eldon replied. He turned to speak to Tamsin, then gathered Owen into his arms.

Ryan thought he could read the little girl's reply: *I'm scared.*

So am I, Ryan thought. If Eldon fell again on the way back across he might lose hold of the little boy. He hoped Eldon wasn't thinking about that right now.

Eldon knotted the ends of the emergency blanket around Owen's neck and waist to secure it. Then he gathered the child to his chest. The little boy wrapped his arms around Eldon's neck and his legs around his broad chest. He needed both hands free to grip the safety line, and would have to trust the boy not to let go. He grimaced as the icy water lapped at his shins, but focused on moving forward and staying upright. Halfway across, Owen began to wail, a pitiful keening Ryan could hear over the current.

The trip back across the water seemed much faster than the journey across. When Eldon and Owen reached the shore, Ryan took the boy from him and Tony helped Eldon stagger out of the water as Sheri set off toward the little girl. "Get into some dry clothes," Tony said. "That's an order. There's some in the back of the Beast."

Ryan carried Owen, who was silent now, shivering and blue-lipped, up to where an ambulance and two paramedics waited, then hurried back down in time to meet Sheri coming out of the water with Tamsin. The little girl was in better shape than her brother, able to stand on her own, one hand clutching the emergency blanket wrapped around her. She stared back across the river at the crushed SUV, which the other volunteers were attacking with the Jaws of Life. "Is my mama going to be okay?"

"She hit her head and she needs to go to the hospital," Ryan said. "That's all I know right now."

"When the car landed in the river, my seat belt broke,"

she said. "I tried to go for help, and thought I should take Owen with me, but we got stuck on this rock."

He shuddered to think of this little girl fighting through that icy current when Eldon had had such a hard time. But he knew from previous rescues that people, even children, could do amazing things when charged with fear and adrenaline.

Tony and Sheri met Ryan on his way back after he had carried Tamsin to meet her brother at the ambulance. "Tamsin told me their grandmother lives in Eagle Mountain," Sheri said. "We're going to call her to come and get them. Later tonight she can take them to see their mother in the hospital."

Another set of rescuers was bringing the children's mother up to road level on a stretcher. The sheriff's deputies had closed off a section of the highway so the medical helicopter could land.

Ryan continued to the riverbank, where he helped Ted coil the ropes and gather the remainder of their gear. "I want to walk down the bank a ways, see if we can spot any big pieces of that SUV," Ted said. "The front right quarter panel and the rear bumper are missing. Something that big gets jammed up in the wrong place, it could cause trouble during melt-off in the spring."

"What are you going to do if you find anything?" Ryan asked. "You don't want to go into that water to rescue a bumper."

"I'll let the wrecker crew know about it," he said. "They can fish it out when they retrieve the SUV." Ted frowned at him. "You don't have to come with me. Go home and get dry."

"I'll come." A man by himself might slip on the icy bank and drown or freeze before the others realized he was missing.

A hundred yards downstream they spotted the quarter panel wedged against a knot of tree roots against the bank. Ted took a picture with his phone. "Let's go a little farther and see if we spot the bumper," he said.

The bank was steep here and thick with snow. Ryan was cursing his decision to help with what he saw as a pointless search when Ted stopped abruptly in front of him. "That doesn't look good," Ted muttered.

"What is it?" Ryan looked past him, to what at first appeared to be a mass of torn limbs and debris caught in the bend of the river.

"Looks like a truck." Ted dug in his pack and pulled out a pair of binoculars. "There's a license plate. I'll see if I can read it."

Ryan could see the truck now, its front end and grille poking out from a tangle of vines.

"Make note of this, will you?" Ted said. "Type it in on your phone or something."

Ryan pulled out his phone and scrolled to the notes ap. "I'm ready."

"966-XXY." He lowered the binoculars. "Why does that sound familiar?"

"Because it's on those posters all over town," Ryan said. "The ones about Mike Traynor's disappearance." He stared at the truck in disbelief. "That's Mike Traynor's truck."

Chapter Fifteen

Monday morning, Deni stood on the side of the highway with Ryan, watching as the wrecker winched her father's truck up from the riverbank. The process was agonizingly slow, the long boom on the oversize crane pulling the truck up a few inches at a time. She could feel the vibrations of the loud diesel motor through the soles of her boots, and she flinched every time the scrape of metal against rock echoed from the canyon. "Almost there!" the winch operator called, and the nose of the truck appeared at the edge of the roadway, like some bug-eyed prehistoric beast emerging from its den.

Deni turned away and buried her face in Ryan's neck. "I can't look," she whispered.

"Mike isn't in there," Ryan said. "We made sure when we found the truck."

She nodded. But she wouldn't be sure until she saw it for herself. The officers who had come to her house Friday evening to confirm that the truck was her dad's had said they wouldn't be able to examine it closely until they pulled it to the roadway. And that couldn't happen until a special wrecker was available on Monday.

Ryan's arms tightened around her. He didn't say anything, but his embrace was comfort enough. He had been her chief support these past few days. He had showed up at the house while she was talking to the deputies—only then did she learn that it was actually him and another search and rescue volunteer who had spotted the truck while cleaning up after another wreck in the area.

The news had stunned her, and raised more questions than it had answered. She had spent an agonizing weekend, and had taken a personal day from school, wanting to be here when they retrieved the truck, yet also not wanting it.

Deputy Wes Landry spoke with the wrecker driver, who finished winching the truck onto his flatbed, then set about securing it. Wes walked over to Deni and Ryan. "The truck is empty," he said. "We'll go over it more thoroughly, but I didn't see any blood on the seats."

She shivered at the image this brought to mind, but nodded. No blood had to be a good sign, right?

"There also aren't any skid marks at the side of the road, as you would expect if the truck slid off the road in an accident," Wes said.

"Could it have been dumped there?" Ryan asked. "Deliberately pushed over the edge?"

"It's possible," Wes commented. "Mike may have done so to confuse the hunt for him."

"Dad really loved that truck," Deni said. "And if he did deliberately destroy it, how did he get away from here? It doesn't make sense."

"If you think of anything that might help us figure this out, let us know," Wes said. How many times had various law enforcement officers said something similar to her in the past few days? As if she was keeping all kinds of secrets from them.

The wrecker pulled away with the truck. "We may have more questions for you once we've had a chance to examine the truck more closely," Wes added.

She nodded. There were always more questions. If only someone could give her answers.

"I have to get to work," Ryan said when Wes had left them. "Will you be okay?"

"Of course."

She dropped him off at the shop, then drove home and crawled into bed, exhausted, but too agitated for sound sleep. But she must have dozed, because she awoke sometime later, disoriented and aching all over, to the sound of distant music. As awareness returned, she realized the music was from her phone. She groped for it on the bedside table and stared at the unfamiliar number on the screen. "Hello?" she answered.

"Hey, Deni, how are you?" said a cheerful female voice. "This is Tammy Patterson."

Deni blinked. Why would the reporter be calling her? She raked a hand through her hair and tried to come fully awake. "What can I do for you, Tammy?"

"I'm working on a story about your dad's disappearance and wanted to include a comment from you."

The words were as effective as ice water splashed over her. She swung her legs over the side of the bed and sat up straight. Tammy was the sole reporter for the

Eagle Mountain Examiner. "Didn't you already run a story about Dad going missing?" she asked. She clearly remembered seeing her dad's picture in the paper.

"This is an update," Tammy said. "I heard his truck was found in the canyon past Ruby Falls. Did that surprise you?"

"Yes," Deni said.

"Have you heard anything from your dad?" Tammy asked. "Do you know what he was up to before he disappeared?"

"No," Deni said.

"You must be terribly worried about him."

"Yes." She couldn't seem to manage more than one-word answers.

"So you don't have any idea what he might have been involved in that led him to just disappear?" Tammy asked.

"I don't know that he was involved in anything," Deni said.

"Have agents Olivera and Ferris spoken with you?" Tammy asked.

Another jolt to the senses. "How did you know about them?" she questioned.

Tammy laughed. "This is a small town, and those two stand out, don't you think? So, did they interview you about your dad?"

"They stopped by, but I couldn't tell them anything," Deni said.

"Is it true your dad was an explosives expert in the army?"

"Where did you hear that?" Deni asked.

"Is it true?"

She tried to collect herself. "That was a long time ago. Obviously, before I was born."

"Mike was pretty upset about the Zenith Mine reopening, wasn't he?" Tammy asked. "And we have on file a letter to the editor he wrote about the ice-climbing festival having a negative environmental impact on Caspar Canyon."

Deni said nothing. The silence between them stretched. "I have to go now," Deni said. "Goodbye."

She hung up before the reporter could say anything further. She tossed the phone aside and debated crawling back under the covers. But she was fully awake now, and too agitated to sit still.

A hot shower and a large cup of coffee later, she was feeling more human, though her stomach churned whenever she replayed the conversation with Tammy in her head. The reporter had obviously connected her father with the bombings. Well, who wouldn't? On paper, her dad looked guilty.

But how could she ever believe the man she loved so much would do something so horrible?

Better to think about questions she could answer. What was she going to do for the rest of the day? She could clean house or grade papers—perpetual items at the top of every to-do list.

Or she could try to find out more about her dad—the life he lived when she wasn't around.

You might find out things you don't want to know an inner voice warned her.

She ignored the voice, and headed for Rouster's Coffee Roasters. She opted to walk, thinking the exercise would be good for her. Dressed in jeans and boots, and a warm sweater and parka, she could appreciate the brisk winter air. Eagle Mountain's Main Street was busy with a mix of locals and tourists, with a line outside the Cake Walk Café, and a family group emerging from the outdoor shop with rented snowshoes, ready for an outing on a local trail.

The part of town where the coffee roaster was located was quieter. She smelled the rich scent of roasting coffee when she was still a block away, and was relieved to see Rouster's old truck parked in the lot. He raised his eyebrows when he saw her at the door. "Back so soon?" he asked. "Are you planning to take your dad's place as my coffee buddy?"

She followed him into the barnlike space where the coffee roaster gave out a welcome warmth. "I wanted to ask you to describe my dad's friend Al," she said. "I never met him."

"Well, now." Rouster shoved his ball cap farther back on his head. "He was pretty average height and weight. About your dad's age, or maybe a few years younger. He had a bit of a belly on him, but that's not so uncommon." He patted his own modest paunch. "I guess the only thing distinctive about him was he had a big bushy beard. I asked him if he was raising chipmunks in that nest." He chuckled. "I don't think he appreciated the joke."

"Did he wear glasses?" she asked, remembering Glenda's description.

"Yeah, he did. Plastic frames, with a black-and-brown pattern."

"Glenda Nassib described a man like that as attending the protests she organized," Deni said. "Only she said his name was Alex."

Rouster nodded. "Maybe that was his full name, but Mike just called him Al."

"What kind of vehicle did he drive?" she asked, and braced herself to hear Al drove a black pickup.

"I don't know that, either. They came here in your dad's Jeep." He checked some gauges on the coffee roaster and made a few adjustments. "Does that help any?"

"I don't know," she admitted. "I've been trying to find Al, to ask him about my dad, but I haven't been having much luck."

"I'm sorry I couldn't be more helpful," Rouster said.

She walked slowly back toward Main, debating her next step. As long as she was out here talking to people about her father, she felt as if she was doing something to help him. If she went home the worries would close in. The problem was, she couldn't think of anyone else to talk to. She decided to prolong her outing a little longer by stopping in to Mo's for lunch. Their homemade soup sounded good on a cold day like today.

The pub was busy, so she ended up sitting at the bar. When the bartender, an older woman with curly blond hair, topped off her water glass, Deni asked, "Did Mike Traynor come in here much?"

The woman eyed her warily. "Are you a reporter or something?"

"I'm Mike's daughter." She wiped her hand on her napkin and held it out. "Deni Traynor."

"Cherise Rodriguez," the woman said. "And yeah, Mike came in here off and on. Not enough that I'd call him a regular, but maybe once every week or so."

"Did he come in alone or with someone else?" Deni asked.

"Mostly alone." Cherise paused, then added, "The last couple of times I saw him, he was with another man about his age. I didn't know him."

"What did he look like?" Deni leaned forward, as if she might miss something if she didn't focus every sense on Cherise.

"Bearded guy with glasses." Cherise shrugged. "I didn't really pay attention beyond that." She leaned closer over the bar and lowered her voice. "A couple of federal agents came in here yesterday, asking about your dad," she said. "I told them the same thing. Mike came in here for a beer sometimes, but he never stood out. What kind of trouble is he in?"

"I don't know," Deni admitted.

Cherise moved on to wait on another customer and Deni's appetite vanished; she paid for her meal and the tip, then went back out onto the sidewalk. The temperature was dropping, clouds building up overhead. She zipped her parka up to her neck. Was Dad camped out somewhere in this weather, or was he far away from here, perhaps even someplace warm?

She turned her attention from the weather to the buildings around her. Was there anyone else here she should talk to? Anyone who might have information about her father? It sounded as if agents Olivera and Ferris were already doing a thorough job of reaching out to everyone who might have come in contact with Mike. Maybe she should leave them to their job and trust that whatever they found out about her dad would be the truth.

Two doors down, a man stepped from the outdoor store. He turned toward her, a middle-aged man of average height with a black knit cap pulled down to his ears. Their gazes momentarily locked and recognition jolted her. This was the man from the yurt. She started walking faster, but he turned abruptly and strode away, lengthening the distance between them with surprising speed. "Wait!" she called, and began to run.

The man ducked into the alley between a boutique and the Nugget Hotel, but before Deni could go after him, she collided with a man on the sidewalk.

"I'm so sorry," she said, apologizing as she moved away from him and righted herself.

But the man kept hold of her arm. "Where are you going in such a hurry?" Agent Olivera asked, his gaze boring into her.

"I'm going home." She tried to wrench away from him, but he held firm.

"We need to talk to you," Olivera said, though he appeared to be alone at the moment. Maybe he meant *we* in the sense of the whole ATFE. "We have more questions."

"I don't have anything else to tell you," she said.

"We've been talking to people," Olivera informed

her. "They all say you and your father were close. You spent a lot of time together."

She would have said the same thing, before her dad disappeared. She met Agent Olivera's gaze with a direct look of her own. "Do you have any children?" she asked.

"Don't try to change the subject. My personal life is none of your concern."

"I asked because if you did have children, you would know that a parent doesn't tell their child everything. My dad is a loving father to me, but that's the only side of him I really see."

"I don't believe you," he said. "And if we find out you're keeping information from us about your father's whereabouts or illegal activities, we can arrest you as an accessory to his crimes. You and your boyfriend, too."

"Ryan doesn't have anything to do with my dad."

"Are you sure? Maybe the two of them are working together. They could compare notes on their time in prison."

She stared. Nothing this man said made sense.

"You didn't know Ryan Welch had a record did you?" Olivera asked. "We're going to be taking a much closer look at him. You tell him so, the next time you see him."

Ryan? In prison? She couldn't believe it, but would Olivera lie about something like that? She tried to pull away from him, but when he didn't release her she said, softly but firmly, "And as far as I know, neither has my father. You need to let me go before I scream and start making a scene in front of people who know me. They don't know you and they might not appreciate a stranger assaulting a local schoolteacher who was minding her own business on the sidewalk." She wasn't certain of that, but she saw the hesitation in Agent Olivera's eyes.

He released his hold on her and stepped back. "We'll be talking to you again," he said. "In a more official capacity, where you can't just walk away."

A chill shuddered through her as she turned her back on him and hurried away. Did they have proof that linked her father to the bombs, or only suspicions? And what about Ryan? She had trusted him with all her doubts and fears about her dad, but she realized now he had told her very little about himself. He had never hinted that he had been in trouble with the law. What else was he hiding from her?

AT WORK TUESDAY MORNING, Ryan was cutting blanks for a new batch of longboards. It was a mostly automated process, which left room for his mind to wander. He was waiting to hear from Bud O'Brien about the extent of damage to his truck, but he didn't have hopes of hearing anything good. The truck was so old he had been carrying only liability insurance on it, so he doubted he would get much of anything from his insurance company. For now, he could walk or take his bike to most places he needed to go, but he would have to catch a ride to any search and rescue scenes, and trips into the backcountry were out unless he went with friends who drove.

The last few minutes before the truck rolled kept replaying in his mind. The sight of that black pickup bearing down on him would haunt him for months to come, he was sure, and the feeling of helplessness when the truck went over still made him break out in a cold sweat.

The automated plasma cutter beeped to indicate it had completed the cut and Ryan hit the button to shut it down, removed the completed blank and set it aside, then inserted another piece of fiberglass. Once all the blanks were cut, he or someone else would move on to sanding and shaping them. They would be painted, varnished and then the hardware attached. The result would be a completed longboard, to be sold online and at stores that catered to skateboarders and other outdoor enthusiasts.

Ryan forced his mind away from the truck. He couldn't do anything to change what had happened, and worrying about the future wasn't going to accomplish anything, either. Better to focus on what was going on in his life right now, which meant Deni. In a very short time, she had become a lot more important to him than he would have imagined. The two of them would have probably hit it off no matter what—he had sensed that from the first morning he spotted her in the coffee shop. But the ways the recent bombings had touched both of their lives, as well as the search for her father, had drawn them even closer together.

He hadn't meant for this to happen. After the way his last serious relationship had turned out, he had decided he was better off remaining single. But that was a lonely way to live, and after he had met Deni, he had told himself they could take things slowly. They would get to know each other, then he would tell her about his past. Maybe she would be able to see beyond that to the man he was now.

But there was nothing slow about the way their relationship had progressed. And he could never find the right moment to tell her everything she needed to know. "By the way, I spent two years in prison because I was really stupid" wasn't the easiest conversation opener.

The door to the shop opened and two men in dark overcoats entered.

The business owner, Xander Kellogg, emerged from his office at one side of the workshop. "The workshop isn't open to the public," he said.

"We're not the public." Agent Olivera pulled out his ID and showed it to Xander. "We need to speak to Ryan Welch."

Xander sent Ryan a questioning look. "Is something wrong?" he asked.

"I'm working," Ryan said, and turned back to the plasma cutter. "I don't have time to talk to you now."

Agent Olivera stepped in front of him. "This won't take long." He looked over Ryan's shoulder to Xander. "You can go back to work, sir. We'll only be a moment."

Xander looked as if he wanted to protest, but apparently thought better of it. He went back into his office, but left the door open.

Agent Ferris joined his partner next to the plasma cutter. "We stopped by the garage and got a look at your truck," Ferris said. "You're lucky to walk away from an accident like that."

"How did you know about the accident?" Ryan asked.

"We were up at Mike Traynor's cabin and ran into a couple of sheriff's deputies. They told us what happened," Olivera said. "Do you have any idea who ran you off the road?"

"No. It happened so fast. I didn't get a look at the driver of the truck, or have time to check the license plate."

The two agents exchanged glances. Did they think he wasn't telling the truth? "Did you see any sign of Traynor at his cabin?" Ferris asked.

"No," Ryan answered. "Deni and I went up there, hoping to find some clue as to where her father might be, but we didn't find anything."

"Maybe Traynor didn't like you up there, snooping around," Olivera said. "Maybe he's the one who ran you off the road."

Ryan stared. "Mike's daughter was a passenger in my truck," he said. "Why would Mike want to hurt her?"

"Maybe he didn't know she was in there. Or, more likely, he didn't care."

Ryan shook his head. He didn't know Mike well, but he knew how Deni felt about her father. She would never believe he had tried to harm her. "I saw Mike's truck in the river past Ruby Falls," he said. "It wasn't the vehicle that ran us off the road."

"Maybe he got a new ride," Ferris conjectured.

"He hadn't been at the cabin," Ryan said. "No one had been there in a long time."

"We think he's hanging out somewhere nearby, keeping an eye on the place," Olivera said.

"Do you have any proof of that?" Ryan asked.

Instead of answering, Olivera leaned against the plasma cutter and folded his arms across his chest. "I understand your girlfriend probably wants to protect her father, but she'll be helping him more by telling us what she knows. Keeping secrets is only going to get more people killed."

Anger flared. "Deni isn't keeping secrets," he said. "If she knew where her father was, she would tell the sheriff."

"But you don't tell all your secrets, do you?" Olivera asked.

Ice formed in the pit of Ryan's stomach. "I don't know what you're talking about," he said.

"We know you did two years inside for credit card fraud," Olivera said. "But you didn't tell Deni that, did you?"

He opened his mouth to ask if they had told her, but he never got the words out. The building shuddered as a reverberation like loud thunder blotted out all other sound. Xander staggered out of his office. "What was that?" he asked, wide-eyed.

Agents Olivera and Ferris were already racing for the door. "It's another bomb," one of them called. Then the lights went out, plunging the room into darkness.

Chapter Sixteen

Home again, Deni paced. She replayed the conversation with Agent Olivera over and over in her head, then moved on to reviewing all her interactions with Ryan. He had seemed less shocked than she had by the revelation that her father had a record for a long-ago crime. He had pointed out that having done time didn't make Mike a bad person.

Was this because he didn't want her to think *he* was a bad person? She didn't think that. But failing to tell her this big, important thing about himself didn't exactly make him a good person, either.

She took out her phone, intending to text Ryan, to ask him to come see her when he got off work. But before she could start typing, what she thought at first was thunder shook the house. Then the wail of sirens filled the air. She ran out onto her porch and saw black smoke filling the sky in the direction of Main Street. "It's another bomb!" Her neighbor across the street stood in her front yard, waving her phone.

"No!" Deni gasped. She stared at the smoke pouring into the sky, wondering if she was asleep and this was a nightmare. But you didn't think that in dreams, did you? "Where?" she asked, as the neighbor turned to go back inside.

"Downtown. At the Nugget Hotel."

Deni clutched her stomach, physically ill. Her father had protested the hotel's proposed expansion—but a lot of people had done that. That didn't mean he was responsible for this. She wanted to believe that, but without him here to defend himself, that was getting harder and harder.

She went back inside and stared at her phone. Who could she call to find out what was going on?

She texted Ryan. RU OK? I heard there was another bomb.

He replied almost immediately. She pictured him with his phone in his hand. Maybe he had been about to call her. I'm fine, he texted. SAR responding to scene. Talk later.

She wanted to call him, to hear his voice tell her everything was going to be okay. But he would be busy, trying to help whoever had been injured in the bombing. Another wave of nausea hit her at the thought.

She pulled up Twitter and began scrolling until she found a thread about the bombing. People were tweeting from the scene. *One wall of the hotel is gone!* read one post, followed by a string of responses condemning whoever had done this.

She didn't know how long she stood there, transfixed by the messages scrolling across the screen from people describing the damage and others speculating on the cause. A knock on the door startled her.

Deputy Jamie Douglas stood on the doorstep. Deni had always liked Jamie, who was the only woman on the force. But seeing Jamie now filled her with dread. Reluctantly, she opened the door. "Hello, Deni," Jamie said. "May I come in? I need to ask you some questions."

Deni opened the door wider and led the way into the living room. "I heard about the bombing," she said. "It's terrible." She sat on the end of the sofa.

Jamie settled into the chair across from her. "Someone said they saw you downtown this morning," she stated.

"Yes."

"What were you doing?"

The question annoyed her. It was a Tuesday morning. She could have been buying groceries or getting coffee with a friend. Jamie must have seen her irritation. "There's a reason I'm asking—I promise," she said.

"I was talking to people who might have known my dad," Deni said. "I'm trying to find out where he's gone and what he was doing in the days leading up to his disappearance."

"You should leave that to law enforcement."

"He's my dad. If it was your father, wouldn't you want to know?"

"Did you learn anything?"

"There's a guy named Al, or Alex, that my dad supposedly hung out with. Rouster Wilson and Cherise, the bartender at Mo's, saw them together. And Glenda Nassib. She says they met at the Zenith Mine protest.

The sheriff already knows about this. Except the bartender. I talked to her today."

Jamie nodded and made notes in a small notebook. "Anything else?"

"Agent Olivera stopped me while I was in town today. I mean, he grabbed me and wouldn't let me go. I already told them I don't know where my dad is or what might have led him to leave, but they won't believe me."

"Where was this, that he stopped you?" Jamie asked.

"In front of the boutique on Main."

"That's right by the Nugget Hotel, isn't it?"

Deni blinked. "It is. I hadn't thought of that."

"What were you doing there?"

"I was just walking. I had come from Mo's and I was trying to think where to go to next."

"And Agent Olivera stopped you to talk to you."

"He grabbed me and started accusing me of helping my dad. He all but called me a liar."

Jamie's expression never changed. "Someone said they saw you coming out of the alley next to the hotel," she said.

Who were these people reporting on her movements? "I wasn't in the alley," she said. "I looked down the alley because I thought I saw the man who lived in the yurt near my dad. I wanted to talk to him, but when I called out to him, he ducked down the alley."

"What man are you talking about?" Jamie asked.

"The sheriff knows about him. Yesterday, Ryan and I stopped by his yurt and asked if he had seen my dad. It's just past my dad's cabin, at the next turnoff. He answered the door and wasn't very friendly. He wouldn't tell us his name, and he said he didn't know Dad. The sheriff said the yurt belongs to a man who lives somewhere else and only uses it in the summer."

"Why did you want to talk to him when you saw him in town?" Jamie asked.

"I wanted to ask him about the truck that tried to run us down after we visited the yurt. You know about that, right? Ryan's truck was wrecked and we could have been killed."

Jamie looked at her notebook again. "Can you describe him?"

Even as Deni described him, she realized how vague she sounded—he was average height, clean-shaven, middle-aged, wearing a black knit cap. That description could apply to almost anyone.

"Did you see anyone else near the hotel?" Jamie asked. "Anyone who was acting suspiciously?"

"No."

"Did you see your father anywhere near the hotel this morning?" Jamie questioned.

"No. I haven't seen him at all in weeks. I haven't heard from him. I don't know anything. How many times do I have to keep repeating that?"

"This is a very serious crime."

As if Deni needed anyone to point that out to her. "You're saying you think my father did this."

"I'm saying we would like to talk to him."

"So would I."

Jamie closed the notebook and stood. "Let us know if you think of anything."

That familiar phrase she was growing sick of hearing. She stood also. "What can you tell me about the bomb at the hotel?" she asked as she followed Jamie toward the front door. "Were many people hurt?"

"They were still searching for people when I came here," Jamie said. "Though I know there were already two fatalities."

Jamie left. Deni locked the door after her and leaned against the wall. The sheriff hadn't wasted any time after the bombing, sending someone to question her. People were watching her. Suspecting her. This place where she had always been at home suddenly felt as if she didn't belong.

In Ryan's time with Eagle Mountain Search and Rescue, he had responded to some terrible emergencies: multiple-car accidents, a gas boiler explosion at a home that had killed three people, and body recoveries on the sides of mountains. But nothing had prepared him for the scene at the Nugget Hotel. Half of the brick building, which had originally been built in the 1890s, had been reduced to rubble, and even before SAR arrived on the scene, people were working to free guests and employees who were trapped in the wreckage.

"This portion of the building held the pool and the gift shop, with a couple of offices over that." Tony briefed them on the sidewalk outside the hotel. "We don't know how many people could be trapped in here, though the manager says less than a dozen—maybe as few as five or six. We know the woman who managed the gift shop was closest to the blast and was killed instantly. A guest who was in the gift shop at the time was blown clear of the blast and died from her injuries. Our priority right now is anyone living. If you find a body, mark it for retrieval later."

"This isn't the kind of urban rescue we train for," Austen said.

"Our job is to assist paramedics and law enforcement," Tony said. "We've got plenty of medical personnel on the scene and the sheriff's department has sent for a couple of search and rescue dogs. The rules are the same as any other rescue—guard your own safety first. The part of the building that hasn't come down could be unstable."

They moved into the scene, joining sheriff's deputies, highway patrol officers, firefighters and others who were combing through the wreckage. At the center of the scene was a large depression Ryan realized was the pool. He started to move away from this when someone shouted they had found a survivor. He and Danny rushed to assist and discovered a boy clinging to the end of a steel girder that extended halfway into the deep end of the pool. "Help! Somebody help!" the boy shouted.

"We're here to help." Ryan lay on his stomach at the edge of the pool, alongside the girder. Chunks of brick and concrete half filled the pool between him and the boy, an unstable soup of jagged edges. Other sections of roof had collapsed into the pool, leaving only a narrow space above the water in which to maneuver. "I'm Ryan. What's your name?"

"Jameson," the boy said. "Jameson Scoville."

"How old are you, Jameson?" Danny asked.

"I'm nine."

"Are you hurt?" Danny asked.

"No. But I don't know how much longer I can hold on. The water's over my head here."

"Hang on a little longer. We're going to get you out," Ryan said.

"What happened?" the boy asked.

Ryan bent lower, his face right at the water level. Through a gap in the rubble, he could see part of the boy's face—part of his cheek and one eye, wide with fear. "A bomb exploded," Ryan said. "Where were you when that happened?"

"I was in the pool, under water. I was trying to touch the bottom. My sister was with me. Do you know where she is? And my mom! My mom was in a chair on the side of the pool. Is my mom okay?"

"We'll find out for you," Ryan said. "You just hang on." He sat up and looked at Danny. "He's about ten feet from the edge here," he said, lowering his voice so that maybe the boy wouldn't hear. "We need to clear a path to him."

Danny surveyed the area. "We need to get rid of this debris, but we can't risk dislodging this beam. It's what's keeping him up."

"Does anyone know about the mom and sister?" Ryan looked around them.

"Don't know." Danny keyed his radio and called for Tony. The SAR commander answered, and Danny explained the situation. "We need a lot of people over here to start shifting this debris," he said.

Seconds later a dozen volunteers gathered and formed a line to move chunks of concrete and metal out of the water. If a piece of the wreckage was too big to remove, they tried to push it aside. "We don't have to get everything out," Ryan instructed. "We just have to clear a path to get to the boy."

While volunteers worked to clear debris, another group began securing the fallen beam that extended into the water. As soon as it was deemed stable, Ryan looped a coil of rope around his shoulders and crawled out on the edge of the beam. As it dipped beneath his weight, a groan rose up from those gathered around, but after a few inches of movement, the beam stabilized, and he was able to advance toward the boy. "Jameson, how are you doing?" he called.

"I'm scared," a shaky voice answered.

"You're doing great," Ryan said. "I'm headed your way. I'm going to try to move aside some of the stuff that's hanging over your head, so get as low as you can to the water, okay?"

"Okay."

Ryan leaned over and grasped a chuck of concrete twice the size of his head. His injured arm protested at the movement, but he clenched his teeth and ignored it. Even so, he was unable to shift the obstacle.

"Try this." He turned and saw a firefighter, extending a garden hoe toward him. "We've been using this to rake stuff out of the way," the woman said.

Ryan took the hoe and found he could use it to roll and push debris aside. Other volunteers continued to lift out chunks of wreckage. Someone had found a winch and was employing it to haul even larger pieces to the edge of the pool. Fifteen minutes passed, with Ryan periodically calling to Jameson, who sounded more and more frantic. "I can't hold on much longer," he said.

"Just a little longer," Ryan said. But even as he said this, Jameson cried out. There was a splash, like something heavy landing in the water. "Jameson?" Ryan called. "Jameson!"

No answer. Ryan stared at the spot where the boy should be. He could make out patches of clear water now, and through one of them he spied a dark shadow sinking toward the bottom.

He slipped into the water, and immediately scraped his upper arm on a twisted chunk of blackened metal. As he dodged this, a shard of broken glass caught at his shirt. He was forced to dive to avoid the floating debris, and scanned the pool for some sign of the boy.

Movement caught his attention and he realized it was Jameson, legs kicking furiously as he tried to surface, but he had drifted to a part of the pool still clogged with debris. Ryan headed toward him. He tried to catch the boy's attention, but Jameson was too frantic, so Ryan was forced to wrap his arms around the struggling child and drag him back toward the beam. Jameson fought, kicking and scratching, and Ryan's chest ached with the need to breathe. When the beam was in reach, he let go of everything but the boy's hand, and dragged himself onto the beam.

Hands reached out, pulling him up, and the boy with him. Danny and Tony and the firefighter hauled him up and to the edge of the pool, where he lay panting, the boy beside him.

"I'm fine," he protested, and pushed Tony away and sat up. Danny and Cassie bent over Jameson, who was very still and pale.

"Jamie!" A petite blond woman, her flowered tankini streaked with blood, rushed to them. She held a little girl in a pink swimsuit in her arms.

Just then Jameson coughed, and the paramedics rolled him onto his side in time for him to vomit up a rush of pool water. The woman crouched beside him, the girl balanced on her hip. "Jamie!" she called again, and touched his face.

"I'm okay, Mom," he said, and tried to sit up, but Danny pressed him back down.

"Not so fast, tiger," he said. "Let's check you over and make sure you're okay first."

Ryan thought the boy would be fine. He stood and looked around to see where he could help next. The pool was much clearer now, and he could make out the remains of the tables and chairs that had once dotted this atrium. "You need to have that cut dressed." Tony moved alongside him and began cleaning the wound in question.

"I didn't even feel it," Ryan said, watching as blood dripped onto the cracked tile.

"Adrenaline," Tony said. He finished cleaning the wound and laid on a gauze pad. "I don't think you need stitches. You're up on your tetanus shots, right?"

"Yeah." It was a requirement for search and rescue work.

Sheriff Travis Walker approached. "All the guests and employees of the hotel are accounted for, along with the people in the gift shop," he said. "I'm ordering everyone out of here before someone else gets hurt."

"Do they have any idea who did this?" Tony asked.

Travis shook his head. "There's a good chance it's the same person who set the other three bombs," he said. "We'll know more once the bomb squad goes over everything."

Do you think it's Mike Traynor? Ryan wanted to ask, but he didn't.

"Whoever is doing this, they had better hope you catch him before someone else does," Austen said. "People are pretty furious about these attacks."

Travis looked grim, but didn't comment. Ryan thought of Deni. What if her dad was guilty? He wanted to be there for her, but how did you help someone through something like this?

DENI CONTINUED TO check the Twitter thread about the bombing, until everyone had been accounted for and the conversation transitioned to speculation about the identity of the bomber. She shut down the app, not wanting to see her father mentioned. She paced the floor, hating this feeling of powerlessness. She couldn't do anything to help the people who had been affected by the bombing, she couldn't stop this from happening again and she couldn't reach her father to find out if he was involved, and if so, why.

She tried to distract herself with work, but concentrating on student essays proved impossible. She tried to remember if any of her students' parents worked at the hotel. She didn't think so, but what if she was overlooking someone? She went online again to pull up the student directory, but while she was waiting for the site to load, a noise outside startled her. It sounded like someone was on the front porch.

Thinking it must be Ryan, she rushed to check the peephole, but couldn't see anything. It was almost full dark outside, so she flipped on the porch light. Still no one in sight, though the noise continued—someone moving about. "Hello?" she called. "Who's there?"

No answer. A chill swept over her. Someone was definitely out there. She grabbed her phone and punched in Ryan's number. "Hey," he answered. "I was just going to call you, see if you wanted some company."

"Then you're not already here?" she asked, even though she already knew the answer.

"No. I'm at my place. I just got out of the shower."

"Someone is outside, on my front porch," she said, keeping her voice low. "I can hear them, but they don't answer when I call out."

"Can you see them?" he asked.

"No. But I heard footsteps, and moving around."

"Hang up and call 911," he said.

"What if it's just an animal? A big dog or a bear? The sheriff's department already thinks I'm lying to them."

"Bears are supposed to be hibernating right now, and a dog doesn't sound like a human moving around. You said you heard footsteps."

"Yes."

"Call 911," he said. "I'll be over as soon as I can." Then he ended the call.

She stared at her phone, then punched in 911. A female voice answered. "What is the nature of your emergency?"

"There's someone on my front porch," she replied. "They don't answer when I call out to them and they're staying where I can't see them."

She waited for the woman to tell her she was probably imagining things, but she merely asked for a name and address and said she would notify the sheriff's department.

Deni returned to the front door and looked through the peephole again. Nothing. But was that a shadow, there on the edge of the reach of the porch light? Her heart pounded and she stepped back and stared at the lock on the door. Would it hold if someone tried to break in?

Headlights illuminated the street in front of her house, and a sheriff's department SUV pulled to the curb. A tall man got out of the vehicle and Sergeant Gage Walker, the sheriff's brother, started up the walk.

Deni opened the door as he mounted the steps to the porch. "Thank you for coming," she said. "I'm sure I heard someone out here."

Gage nodded, and looked to his right. "Looks like someone wanting to stir up trouble," he said. "Did you get a look at them at all?"

"I never saw anyone, just heard them." She stepped onto the porch, the chill air washing over her, and followed his gaze to the wall beside the door. Someone had spray-painted the side of her house in foot-high letters, the color of fresh blood: KILL THE BOMBER.

Chapter Seventeen

"You need to come back to my place," Ryan said, after the shock of seeing the message from the anonymous tagger had subsided. "It's not safe for you here." He had arrived only moments after Gage and had been horrified at what he found.

Deni looked to Gage, who had stepped back and was photographing the graffiti. "Why would someone do this?" she asked.

"People are pretty upset about these bombs," Gage said.

"But I didn't have anything to do with them," she responded.

"No, but some people think your father did." He tucked his phone back into his pocket and took out a notebook. "To them, you're guilty by association."

She frowned, but he had already turned away, his attention focused on the notebook in his hand. "What time did you hear someone on the porch?" he asked.

"Just a few minutes before I called 911," she said.

"Did you see any cars nearby, maybe parked on the street?" Gage asked. "Anyone hanging around, maybe right before then?"

"I wasn't looking outside before then, and I didn't see any cars or anyone," she said. "Maybe one of my neighbors saw something."

"We'll talk to them," Gage said. He looked around. Snow had started to fall, big flakes drifting through the light from the porch. "This snow is going to cover any tracks your graffiti artist might have made."

She stared at the spray-painted message again. "What am I going to do?"

"The hardware store sells some cleaner that will take off the paint," Gage said. "Though you might have to repaint this part of the house, too." He glanced at Ryan. "In the meantime, it might be a good idea if you went somewhere else for a few days. We'll have a deputy drive by several times each shift to keep an eye on things. Maybe we'll get lucky and catch whoever it was coming back to try again."

Ryan didn't think Gage sounded optimistic. He moved to put his arm around Deni. "There's nothing more you can do tonight," he said. "Why don't you pack a bag and come with me? Cookie can come, too."

Her expression softened. "That's so sweet of you to think of my cat, but Cookie doesn't do well in strange situations. She'll be happier here, as long as I'm not gone too long."

"Will you come to my place, then? At least for the night?"

"Yes. Thanks." She moved away and went inside. When she was gone, Ryan turned to Gage. "Deni hasn't done anything wrong," he said. "She wants to find her dad as much as you do. And she wants these bombings to stop."

"Even if it means arresting her father?" Gage asked.

"At least then more people wouldn't be hurt." He absently rubbed at his arm, which still ached from the afternoon's efforts. "Is Mike Traynor your only suspect?"

"No," Gage said. "We're looking at a lot of people. But Mike is the only one with a background in explosives, and he's the only one who disappeared around the time of the first bombing. That looks suspicious."

"I don't know what to tell you," Ryan said. "Except that Deni hasn't done anything wrong." He stared at the ugly words painted on her house. "She doesn't deserve this."

Gage nodded. "Take her home and keep her safe," he suggested. "We'll keep working things on our end."

Gage called for a team to search the area and question neighbors. Ryan went in search of Deni and found her in her bedroom, a suitcase open on the bed. "I can't think straight," she said. "What should I take with me?"

"Let me help." Together, they assembled clothing and toiletries to last a few days, then collected her student papers and books she needed for her job. By the time they emerged from the house, two deputies were searching the flower beds and yard, though the snow was falling harder now, obscuring everything. Gage nodded to them, then turned back to his officers.

Deni stopped halfway down the walk. "How did you get here?" she asked. "I forgot about your truck."

"I rode my bike." He gestured to the mountain bike

leaning against the banked snow at the side of her driveway.

"At least we can take my car now." She hit the key fob to unlock the vehicle and he retrieved his bike, which just fit in the back, with the rear seat folded down.

Ryan lived in an apartment over an art gallery, three blocks from the snowboard and skateboard manufacturer where he worked. "My landlords remodeled this space as a rental a few years back," he explained as he ushered her inside. "I was lucky to get it."

Though small, the apartment had an open, airy feel, with big windows and high ceilings, white-painted walls and blond wood floors. The clock on the microwave in the galley kitchen showed just after ten o'clock when they walked in. "If you're tired, go on to bed," Deni said. "I'm too keyed up to sleep."

"So am I." He moved to the cabinet and opened it. "Why don't I make some coffee and we can talk?"

She settled at the table and watched him move about, adding coffee to the old-fashioned drip machine, getting out mugs and milk. "Are you hungry?" he asked. "I can make toast."

"Just coffee is fine with me," she said. "You eat if you want."

When the coffee was done, he filled two mugs and brought them to the table. "I'll eat in a minute. Tell me about your day."

She stirred sugar and milk into her mug. "I ran into Agent Olivera downtown," she said.

He had been waiting for this, but that didn't make

it any easier. He froze, his back to her, gathering the courage to turn around.

"He told me you had been in prison," she said. "Is that true?"

He faced her, every muscle still tensed, trying to read her expression. "It's true," he said.

"Why didn't you tell me?" She pushed the coffee cup away. "Didn't you think it was something I would want to know?"

He moved to the table and sat across from her. Her gaze remained locked on him, hurt radiating. "I didn't tell you because I don't tell anyone," he said. "It's in the past and I don't talk about it."

"No one else knows?"

"Xander knows. You have to tell employers if you have a record. Most of them won't hire you when they find out, but Xander was willing to take a chance on me."

"Does the sheriff know?"

"He probably does now. Olivera probably told him if he wasn't already aware." He wanted to reach out and take her hand. Instead, he laced his fingers together. "I didn't tell you because I didn't want you to look at me the way you are now."

She leaned back. "What way is that?"

"Like I'm a bad person. Someone you can't trust."

"I'm just shocked, that's all. And I don't think you're a bad person. But I wish you'd tell me what happened."

He sighed. "The short answer is, I got involved with the wrong person and was stupid. Remember, I told you I worked at a restaurant? There was a waitress there, Tracy. I was 19. She was 25 or 26. I liked her. I thought she liked me. Turned out she was stealing people's credit card information. When she took the card for them to pay, she would take pictures of the fronts and backs of the cards and use it later to order stuff. She had a friend who resold the stuff. Sometimes she sold the credit card information. I found out what she was doing, but she persuaded me to turn a blind eye. She said it wasn't hurting anyone. Then I found out she had been using my phone to take the pictures of the cards most of the time. I kept the phone in my locker while I was working, but she knew the combination. I never thought to look—until the cops who were onto her scam showed me all the evidence against me. Tracy told them the whole scam was my idea, that she only went along because she was afraid of me."

"Oh, Ryan," Deni whispered.

"Don't feel sorry for me," he said. "I was an adult. I should have known better. As it was, my parents paid for a really expensive, really good lawyer and he persuaded the jury that the prosecutors couldn't prove I was the one who planned everything. He portrayed me as the dupe I really was, so I only had to serve a little over two years."

"What happened to Tracy?"

"I don't know and I don't care."

"I'm sorry you had to go through all of that," she said.

"I got what I deserved and I'm not going to make a mistake like that again."

"I believe you." She put her hand over his. "And I

know you're a good person. But I'm glad I know about this, too."

"I was going to tell you," he said. "I just had to work up the nerve."

He turned his hand palm up and laced his fingers with hers. They sat there for a long moment, the silence between them easier. "I want to tell you what happened this morning, before I ran into Agent Olivera," she said.

"I want to hear all about it."

"AFTER YOU LEFT, I couldn't settle down," she said. "I decided to go into town and talk to Rouster again, and anyone else who might have seen my dad with Al. Rouster gave the same description of Al as Glenda gave of Alex, so I think they are the same man. Then I spoke to the bartender at Mo's. She said she had seen Dad in there with Al a few times, but she couldn't tell me any more about him. She said the ATFE agents had been in there, asking about Dad, too."

"They're probably asking about a lot of people," he said.

"Do you really think so?" She shook her head. "Agent Olivera stopped me on the street after I left Mo's. He grabbed my arm and wouldn't let go. He's convinced I know something that I'm not telling him and he wouldn't take no for an answer. He didn't let me go until I threatened to make a scene, but he threatened to arrest me if he found out I was keeping anything from him."

"He's not finding any solid evidence to tie your dad to the bombings if he's making threats like that," Ryan said.

She sipped the coffee, his reassurance soothing her

agitated nerves. "Right before Agent Olivera stopped me, I thought I saw the man we talked to at the yurt," she said. "I called out to him and he ducked down an alley, right by the hotel. I didn't even realize it was by the hotel, but later Deputy Jamie Douglas came to the house to question me. She said someone had seen me right by the hotel not too long before the bomb went off. I tried to tell her about the man in the yurt, but I don't think she believed me."

"Wait a minute," Ryan said. "You were at the hotel? Right before the bomb went off?"

"It was at least a half an hour before the bomb went off, and I was only near the hotel, not even directly in front of it. And I never went inside."

"Was the man from the yurt at the hotel?"

"I don't know," she said. "When I saw him he was walking down the street from that direction. He ducked into the alley. I thought he was trying to get away from me, but maybe he was just taking a shortcut back to wherever he was parked."

"When did Deputy Douglas come to the house?" he asked.

"Right after the bomb went off. Apparently, someone mentioned seeing me at the hotel and the sheriff sent her to talk to me—probably because now I'm a suspect. Maybe they think I planted a bomb for my dad or something."

"It will be easy enough for them to check with Rouster and the bartender at Mo's and confirm that you were talking to them," he said.

"Yes. It's just so…annoying. I keep telling everyone

the same things over and over—that I don't know where my father is or what he's doing—but no one is listening."

"I'm listening," he said, and the warmth in his eyes chased away some of the cold fear that had taken up residence inside her these last few days. "What about you?" she asked. "What did you do today?"

"Agents Olivera and Ferris came to see me at work," he said. "Probably after Olivera talked to you."

"Why did they want to talk to you?" she asked.

"I think they were hoping I'd tell him all your secrets about you and your dad. And you're right—they don't listen to anything they don't want to hear. I told Olivera you were telling the truth and that you didn't know anything about your dad's activities. He suggested I should put pressure on you to confess all—even though I told him you don't have anything to confess. And then the bomb went off and the two of them ran out of there." He sat back in his chair. "And I got a text that search and rescue needed me to report to the hotel."

"Oh no," she said. "I didn't even think of that. What could you do at the hotel?"

"Dig people out of the rubble and administer first aid," he said. "Fortunately, not too many people were in the part of the building where the bomb went off. But two people died, and several others were seriously injured."

"I'm sorry," she said. "That must be hard to deal with."

"It can be." He finished the last of his mug of coffee and set it down with a thump. "But today was a good day. We rescued a little boy." He told her about everyone working together to save Jameson.

"Is that how you got this?" She leaned forward and brushed her fingers across the bandage on his upper arm.

"There was a lot of broken glass," he said. "It's just a cut."

She sat back. "This can't keep happening," she responded. "It's terrifying."

"It makes you wonder where the bomber will strike next," he said.

"Do you have some paper we can write on?" she asked. "I want to make a list of everywhere there has already been a bomb, and see if I can see a pattern."

"Sure." He got up and retrieved a spiral notebook from a drawer, along with a couple of pens. He flipped to a blank page in the notebook and slid it toward her. "The sheriff's department is probably already doing this," he said.

"Yes, but if my dad is behind everything, I probably know him better than anyone." The cops were right about that, at least. "Maybe I will see something they don't—some clue as to what he's trying to accomplish."

Ryan gave her a curious look. "So you don't think he's innocent?"

"I do! At least, I want to. I don't know what to think."

He pulled her close. "Whatever happens, it's on your dad," he said. "It's not your fault and it's not on you."

"I know." She took a deep breath and pulled herself together. "But I can't sit here and do nothing, either. So—back to this list."

She drew lines to divide the page into columns, then began writing down what they knew about the site of each bombing, the result of the bomb and her father's connection to each location. "Grizzly Creek bridge, Caspar Canyon Ice Climbing Area, the Zenith Mine and the Nugget Hotel," she read out loud. "Well, we know that my dad had protested development in all those areas, either by writing letters to the editor of the paper or attending town council meetings where development was discussed."

"And the in-person protests at the Zenith Mine," Ryan said.

She nodded and continued to stare at the list. "Do you see anything else?" he asked.

"The bombings are getting worse." She looked at him. "Does that mean the bombs are getting bigger or the bomber is getting better at placing them to do the most damage?"

"Maybe both?" He leaned over her shoulder to study the list. "What else do the sites have in common?"

"I don't know." She clenched her head in her hands, as if that would make it easier to see what she was missing.

"Where else did your dad complain about or protest?"

She closed her eyes. "I can't think. I didn't pay attention, really. Maybe we can ask Glenda. She organized a lot of protests."

"Then let's do that tomorrow." He rubbed her back. "We're both exhausted. Let's get some sleep."

"All right." She brought her hand up to cover his. "And thank you. For letting me stay here and for being here." *For not leaving when you saw that graffiti written on the side of my house.*

"I'm not going to leave you," he said, as if reading her thoughts. "You're too important to me now."

She thought about what he had told her, about the woman he had fallen for. She had betrayed him in the worst way. It was a wonder he had ever let Deni—a woman whose father was a suspected terrorist—get close to him at all. Did he worry he was making another mistake?

She would do her best to prove he wasn't.

Deni slept fitfully and woke early, disoriented by a dream she had had of her father. He had been calling to her, pleading for help. She had stumbled through a snowy ravine, floundering through drifts and scrambling over icy rocks, his voice lost in a howling wind, then coming from another direction entirely.

She woke in a tangle of blankets, cheeks wet with tears, Ryan sleeping soundly beside her. Careful not to wake him, she slipped out of bed and carried her clothes into the bathroom to dress.

The snow had stopped falling and the sun was rising, the scenery outside the window fresh and peaceful. In the kitchen, she made coffee, then studied the list she had left lying on the kitchen table. Last night, she and Ryan had talked about everything the bomb sites had in common, but this morning, a difference stood out to her. While her father had written letters to the editor or participated in organized protests against the bridge, the mine and the hotel expansion, he hadn't done that for Caspar Canyon. Yes, he had complained about the extra traffic, and the damage to the environment that might result from overuse, but he had never suggested anyone close the canyon to climbing, only that the town should better regulate the activities there. Plus, the other three places where bombs had been placed had been man-made structures the bombs had the potential to damage or destroy. The damage in the canyon had been to nature, and to people. Her father had always talked about protecting the natural beauty of this area, not destroying it.

When Ryan came into the kitchen some time later, he found her bent over the notebook, writing furiously. "Good morning," he said. "What's up?"

She looked up, and brushed a fall of hair out of her eyes. "Hey. I couldn't sleep, so I got up and started studying this list again. I think I figured something out."

He pulled a mug from the cabinet and filled it from the carafe. "What's that?"

She explained about the difference between Caspar Canyon and the other sites. "It's like Glenda said—Dad and the other protesters at the mine and the hotel didn't have anything against the people involved in those projects—they just want to protect the landscape. I think my dad really believed that, too."

Ryan sat across from her and sipped coffee. "That points to your dad not being involved in the bombings, but it doesn't help us find him. And it doesn't give us a clue as to where the next bomb might be."

"I did think of one thing," she said. "Though it's pretty far out there."

He set down his coffee mug. "Let's hear it."

"The town council are the ones who decide on all these projects," she said.

"Right."

She looked at her notebook again. "If you plot the location of the bombs so far, each one is a little closer to downtown. What if that's intentional? What if the bomber's next target is the courthouse, where the council meets?"

Ryan's face registered the shock she had felt when the idea had first occurred to her. "When does the town council meet again?" he asked.

"I checked the town website," she said. "The next meeting is tomorrow night."

"We have to let the sheriff know about this," he said.

"They'll either think I'm imagining things, or they'll believe me and arrest me for having insider knowledge. Or maybe they've already figured this out on their own."

"If I had gone to the police as soon as I figured out what Tracy was up to, I would have saved a lot of people a lot of trouble," he said. "Including myself. Do you want to risk them not knowing, and you being right?"

"No." For the past hour she had wrestled with the question and come to the same conclusion Ryan had.

They had to tell the sheriff. After that, it was in his hands.

She stood. "I'm going to take a shower," she said. "I already called the school and took another personal day."

"Were they upset?" he asked.

"No. The principal actually said he thought that would be a good idea. I imagine news about that graffiti on my house is all over town by now." But she wasn't going to think about that.

"I'll go with you to the sheriff's department," Ryan said.

"Don't you have to work?"

"I can go in late. Xander is pretty laid-back and we're not particularly busy right now."

"Thanks." She told herself she didn't need him to go with her, but she would feel better with him there. Through this whole ordeal, he had been the one person she could count on.

ADELAIDE KINKAID, the office manager at the sheriff's department, studied Ryan and Deni over the tops of red-rimmed bifocals. "The sheriff is a very busy man," she said.

"We won't take much of his time, but this is important," Deni stressed.

Adelaide picked up her phone. "One of the deputies can see you," she said.

"It has to be the sheriff." Deni was polite, but it was clear she wasn't going to back down.

Adelaide replaced the phone in its cradle. "Let me talk to him," she said, and left the room.

"Do you think I should have hired a lawyer to come with me?" Deni asked Ryan, her voice just above a whisper.

"Maybe." Probably. But they didn't have time for that. Not if Deni's theory was true.

Adelaide returned a few moments later. "The sheriff can give you a few minutes," she announced.

Travis was waiting for them behind his desk. He didn't stand to greet them, but his tone was gentle. "What did you need to see me about, Deni?" he asked.

Deni sat in the chair in front of the desk and spread out the chart and other notes she had made.

"I've been trying to think where the bomber might strike next," she said. "I still don't think my father is doing this, but I want to help."

Travis looked at Deni, not the paperwork. "What have you figured out?"

She showed him how each bomb target was closer and closer to the center of town. "If this is some kind of protest against development, then why not target the people who made decisions about that development? And the place where they meet?"

"So you think the next bomb will be at the court-house?" he asked.

"The town council has another meeting there to-morrow night," she said. "I don't know if I'm guessing right, but what if I am?"

"And that's all this is?" Travis asked. "A guess?"

"Yes!"

Ryan rested a hand on her shoulder and felt her trembling. "Maybe you already figured this out and I'm wasting your time," she conceded. "But I wanted to say something, just in case." She gathered her papers and stood.

"Thank you," Travis said. "Are you still sure your father doesn't have anything to do with these bombs?"

"Dad always said he wanted to protect places, not destroy them. And he's not a killer. I can't see it." She shook her head. "But he's my dad, so maybe I don't want to see it. If you're able to catch whoever is responsible, maybe then we'll know."

Travis nodded. "And maybe you've helped. No matter what happens, don't feel bad about that."

"Have you found out any more about the person who ran us off the road?" Ryan asked.

"No," Travis said.

"What about the man we talked to at the yurt?" Ryan asked. "Deni said she saw him in town yesterday, near the hotel."

"We've been looking for him," Travis said. "We contacted the owner of the yurt and he says no one should be there. We stopped by twice and no one was around."

"We really did see him," Deni said. "We didn't make that up."

"I never said you did," Travis replied.

But did he believe that? Ryan wondered. The sheriff was so hard to read, and since Ryan and Deni were the only people who claimed to have seen this mysterious man, he could understand how someone else might think they had made up the story.

"We'll be in touch," Travis said. "Thank you for stopping by." Which was clearly a dismissal.

"What do you want to do now?" Ryan asked when they were on the sidewalk again.

"I want to go back to that yurt," she said. "I want to find the man we talked to and ask him why he ran from me when I saw him Monday. And I want to know what he was doing hanging around the hotel just before that bomb went off."

"If he's involved in this, it might not be safe," Ryan said.

"I'm feeling reckless. Or desperate. At this point, I'm not sure there's much difference between the two." She set off down the sidewalk. Ryan hurried after her. When had he changed from believing he should distance himself from her to knowing he should stick by her? He thought it was probably when Olivera and Ferris had first questioned her. He had been in that position, with no one who believed in him to stand by him. He believed in Deni. He was even beginning to believe in what the two of them could be together.

FRESH SNOW HAD covered the tracks of their previous visit here, and wiped out even the ruts formed by the wrecker that had hauled away Ryan's damaged truck, but someone had traveled this way. They followed a single set of tire tracks up the road. Deni turned her head away from the place where they had been run off the road, fear churning her stomach. She had been half hoping Ryan would try to talk her out of this reckless idea of confronting the man in the yurt, but he hadn't said anything against it, though he had insisted she leave a note for her neighbor, letting her know where they were headed and how the insurance appraiser coming to review the damage to her house might reach her if he stopped by. "With my luck, agents Olivera and Ferris will see the note and decide to come question me again," she had told Ryan.

"It might come in handy to let the man in the yurt know a couple of federal agents are headed his way," Ryan said. "Just in case he turns out to be the man in the black truck who ran us down."

No truck was visible when they pulled into the narrow drive that led to the yurt. No smoke drifted from the stovepipe, and all the windows were shut tight. "It looks deserted," Ryan said, after he had turned Deni's Subaru around and parked with the front of the car facing toward the road.

"Let's get out and look around," Deni said.

Footsteps in the snow led from the front door of the yurt to a cleared area where a vehicle had been parked. "It's a big enough space for a truck," Ryan said.

Deni mounted the steps to the front door and knocked, but there was no answer. "Hello!" she called. "Anybody home?"

"I think he's gone." Ryan joined her on the small front porch. "Remember, the cops said he wasn't here when they tried to talk to him."

"Someone has been here since the snow last night,"

she said, pointing to the tracks. They were large, a man's lug-soled boots.

"Maybe a cop," Ryan said.

"Let's look around a little, as long as we're here," she said.

She didn't know what she expected to find, but walking through the snowy woods felt better than sitting around doing nothing.

She found more tracks around the back of the yurt, a fainter trail that led into the underbrush. "Maybe that goes to an outhouse," Ryan said.

"Maybe," Deni mused. "But this path heads in the direction of my dad's cabin. Maybe there's a spot where we can look down on Dad's place."

They set off down the path, Deni in front, Ryan on her heels, the underbrush so close on either side they could only travel single file. After fifty yards, the trail ended. Not at an outhouse or any kind of scenic viewpoint.

"Why make a trail through the woods that goes nowhere?" Ryan asked.

Deni turned a complete circle, searching around them. Then she looked up and felt a jolt of surprise. "Not nowhere." She pointed up. "He's got a tree house."

That was the only way to describe what sat overhead, well camouflaged in a large fir to the left of the trail. A little shack was built on a platform in the tree, with wooden sides, shuttered windows and a rusting metal roof.

The two of them walked over and stared up at the little building. "How does he get up there?" Deni asked.

"There must be a ladder." Ryan looked around. "There!" He pointed and Deni followed his gaze to another tree, deeper in the woods, and the wooden ladder propped against its trunk.

"Let's see what's up there," she said, and hurried toward the ladder.

Ryan helped her to haul the ladder to the tree house, where it fitted neatly against two notches in the platform on which the little house was constructed. "This is probably trespassing," Ryan said.

"Probably." Deni put her foot on the bottom rung. "But I'm not going to hurt anything. I just want to see."

She climbed to the platform, ignoring the butterflies in her chest. She had always been the good girl, the one who never broke the rules or stepped out of line. All it had taken was the police to start treating her like a criminal for all her scofflaw tendencies to emerge.

She climbed onto the platform and stood. The door to the little house was to her right—not a flimsy home-made portal, but a solid door like she might see on any home. She walked the few steps to it and tried the knob, but the door was locked. Feeling a little foolish, she knocked. "Hello!" she called.

A scuffling noise from inside startled her. Heart pounding, she pressed her ear to the door. "Hello?" she called again. "Is someone there?"

"Help!" The word was muffled, but still distinguishable. "Help!" A man's gravelly voice, the voice from her dream.

She raced to the ladder and looked down at Ryan. "Find something to break down this door," she called. "I think we've found my dad!"

Chapter Eighteen

Several hard blows with the tire iron from Deni's car broke the lock on the tree house door. Ryan shoved open the door, brandishing the tire iron. At first, he saw nothing in the dim light, then a voice broke through the stillness.

"Deni!"

"Dad!" Deni started to run to him, then stopped as the bizarre scene before them registered. A thin, white-haired man balanced precariously on a wooden crate on top of a table with only three of its four legs in place. He gripped the noose around his neck with both hands.

Ryan pulled out his phone and switched on the flashlight ap. Mike Traynor stared at them, eyes wide with terror. "Don't just stand there—cut me down!" he croaked.

Ryan rushed forward to grasp Traynor around the knees and hold him up, just as the table tipped and the crate fell. "See if you can find something to cut this rope," Ryan said as the older man's weight sagged against him.

Deni looked frantically around the room which, except for the broken table, was empty. "Break a window," her father said.

Ryan saw now that the windows, though covered with wooden shutters, did indeed have glass panes. "Careful," he said, as Deni picked up the broken table leg and hurled it at the back window. Glass shattered and a few shards fell to the floor. She picked up one, righted the crate and stood on it to saw at the rope with the broken glass. Agonizing minutes passed until the rope began to fray.

With a groan from the rafters, the rope snapped and Mike and Ryan both fell to the floor.

Deni rushed to them and began helping her father loosen the noose around his neck. "Dad, what is going on?" she asked.

"Water," he gasped, and rubbed at his throat, where the rope had chafed an angry red ring.

"There's some in the car," Ryan said, and went to retrieve it. But a note tacked inside the door stopped him. "Deni," he said, in a warning tone.

She looked up. "What is it?"

"You'd better see for yourself."

She joined him in front of the door. The writing was almost illegible, sloping upward on the page. "I'm sorry about the bombs," it read. "I never meant to hurt anyone. I only wanted to stop all this development." It was signed Mike Traynor.

"Al made me write that." Mike staggered to his feet. "He put a gun to my head—one of my own guns, from the trunk he stole from my house. He said he would shoot me if I didn't do as he said. I was ready to let him do it, but then he threatened you, so I gave in."

"Where is Al?" Deni asked.

"I don't know, but he'll probably be back soon," Mike said.

"Then we need to get out of here." Ryan took his arm. "Can you walk to Deni's car?"

Mike nodded. "I may need a little help, but I can do it."

On the way out, Deni stopped and tore the note from the door. She folded it and tucked it into her pocket. "That might be evidence," Ryan said.

"I'll give it to the sheriff," she promised. "I just don't want anyone finding it and thinking it's real before we have a chance to explain."

"I'm sorry about all this," Mike said as he hobbled between them toward the yurt and Deni's car. "I've been really stupid."

"It's okay, Dad," she said. "I'm so glad to see you."

"Just tell us one thing," Ryan said. "Is there another bomb?"

"I think so," Mike said. "I think he intends it to go off during the town council meeting at the courthouse. He wants everyone to think I did it—that I did all of them."

"Al is responsible for all those bombs?" Deni said. "He just framed you for them?"

"We set the first one at the Grizzly Creek bridge," Mike admitted. "It was just a prank, really, to get people's attention. It wouldn't have gone off—I made sure of that. But then Al wanted to make a real one. I refused. That's when he kidnapped me. I thought I had talked him out of the whole plan. He said we were going on a snowmobile outing, and when he got me alone, he tied me up and imprisoned me in that tree house. He stole my guns from the cabin and used the dynamite I'd intended to use on my spring to make more bombs and put them around town. He'd come back and tell me what he had done, and how everyone would believe I was responsible."

The story was incredible. Ryan might not have believed it, except for the way they had found Mike balanced on that table. "He intended to kill you and make it look like suicide," he said.

"Yes," Mike confirmed. "It's a good thing you came along when you did. I don't think I would have lasted much longer."

"What is Al's full name?" Ryan asked. "And what does he look like?"

"His name is Alex Coggins," Mike said. "He used to have a full beard and glasses, but he shaved off the beard and threw away the glasses after he kidnapped me. He was in the Explosives Division like I was. He served in a different part of the country, so I didn't know him back then, but it was one of the things we had in common. I met him at the protest against the Zenith Mine and we hit it off and started hanging out." He looked at Deni. "It was nice to have a friend to do things with. I guess he really played me."

"Is Al the person who ran us off the road when we came up here to look for you?" Deni asked.

"I don't know about that," Mike said. "But it sounds

like him. He's ruthless when it comes to getting what he wants."

"We found your truck, wrecked in Grizzly Creek," Deni said. "I was so afraid we would find you with it, dead or injured."

"Al did that to throw off anyone who was looking for me," Mike said. "And maybe to make it harder for me to get away. He said people would think I wrecked the truck on purpose in a suicide attempt."

"Oh, Dad." Deni hugged him close.

"Why is he blowing up everything?" Ryan asked.

"Because he can, I guess," Mike said. "Something isn't right with him. I noticed it pretty early on, but I just told myself everyone has their quirks." He hung his head.

Deni took a firmer hold on his arm. "We're almost to the car, Dad," she said. "You can tell the sheriff what you know. You'll help prevent more people being killed."

Ryan wondered if Deni realized her father could be charged for his part in the first bomb, the one at the Grizzly Creek bridge. He might even be treated as an accessory to the other bombings. He looked across at her, and decided having her dad back and safe meant more than any worries about his future.

They reached the back of the yurt and Mike swayed and made a moaning sound.

"Dad, are you okay?" Deni asked. "What's wrong?"

"Just...don't feel so good." He closed his eyes, his face gray. After all he had been through, was he having a heart attack?

Ryan eased the older man up against the side of the yurt. "Are you in pain?" he asked.

"Just...dizzy." He leaned against the yurt. "Just give me a minute to catch my breath."

Ryan felt at Mike's throat for a pulse. A little rapid but strong. "Are you having any chest pains?" he asked. "Any numbness in your arms?"

"No. Just...weak."

No telling when he had last eaten, or how long he had been straining to balance on his precarious perch upon the uneven table.

"We'll rest here a minute, then get you to the car," Ryan said. Maybe he and Deni could form a chair to carry the older man.

"Someone's coming!" Deni whispered.

Ryan froze, ears straining, then he heard the crunch of tires on snow. He swore and looked around for anywhere they might hide.

"It's Al," Mike said. "He's coming back to see if I'm dead yet."

The underside of the yurt was enclosed, so no hiding place there. They would have to sprint twenty yards to the cover of the woods, through thick snowbanks. Mike would never manage, and the snow would make their retreat obvious. If they retraced their steps to the tree house, Al would find them there.

"My car is parked right out front," Deni whispered. She moved in closer to Ryan. "He'll know we're here."

"Leave me and go," Mike said. "He'll be too distracted by me to go after you. You can circle around to your car and I'll keep him occupied until you get away."

"No," Deni protested. She clung to his arm. "I won't leave you."

Ryan took hold of Mike's other arm. "She's right. We won't leave you."

The vehicle stopped, and a car door slammed. They stood frozen, unable to go anywhere without being seen.

Seconds later, the clean-shaven man in the black knit cap they had first seen here at the yurt came around the side. He carried a large handgun, and focused it on Deni.

"Al, you leave her alone!" Mike struggled, but Deni and Ryan held him firm.

"I'm glad to see you both," Al said to Ryan and Deni. "You've saved me the trouble of looking for you."

"What are you going to do with us?" Deni asked. Ryan wished she hadn't. He didn't really want to know Al's plan, which probably involved the gun in his hand.

"You'll find out soon enough." He jabbed the gun toward her. "But first, we're all going to go back to the tree house. And this time, I promise you won't leave."

AL FORCED THEM at gunpoint to climb into the tree house. Deni climbed behind her father, watching as he took each shaky step. He must be exhausted—and thirsty. They had never made it to the car, and the water he had asked for. Ryan was in front of her father. What did he think about being caught up in such a nightmare?

Al moved right behind her, jabbing her with the pistol every few steps, as if she needed reminding what was at stake here. When they reached the platform, Al

scowled at the broken lock on the door, but said nothing. "Get inside," he ordered.

They filed in. Al turned to Mike. "Get that rope and
tie up these two." He gestured with the gun to Deni and
Ryan. "Back to back. And do it up tight. I'll check."

Mike shuffled to the noose and picked it up. He
looked much older to Deni, and defeated. She would
have never thought her father would let anyone order
him around this way. Then again, the gun in Al's hand
was a powerful persuader. "How do you want me to
do it?" Mike asked.

"You two, sit on the floor, arms linked and backs
together," Al said.

Ryan met Deni's gaze. He didn't look defeated,
more—resigned. He sat, and she lowered herself to
the floor also, then sat with her back pressed to his,
knees up. "Link arms," Al ordered.

They did as he asked, and her father knelt beside
them with the rope. "I'm sorry about this," he muttered.

"It's okay, Dad," she said.

Mike looped the rope around them several times,
then double knotted it over Ryan's stomach. Al bent
to tug at the rope with one hand, the other keeping
the gun focused on Mike. "That should do," he said,
and straightened. He looked around the single room.
"Where's the suicide note you wrote before?"

Mike blinked at him, looking confused. "I don't
know."

Al struck him hard across the face, leaving the red
imprint of his hand. Mike staggered back, clutching
his face.

"I tore up the note and threw it away," Deni said. "It was all lies."

"We don't need a note," Al said. "It will be clear enough to the authorities when they show up. Mike shot both of you, then put the gun to his own head, after his last bomb destroyed the courthouse and everyone in it."

"You don't have enough dynamite to do that," Mike said.

"I was at the Zenith Mine, remember? The thing about mines is, they have lots of explosives. I was able to help myself to everything I needed. Of course, people will think you stole it, when you planted that second bomb."

He turned to Deni. "You were there, weren't you? Maybe people will think you helped your old man. Like father, like daughter, huh?" He laughed, the sound sending a shiver down Deni's spine. She wanted to fling herself at him, to scratch out his eyes, but the rope bound her so tightly to Ryan she could scarcely draw a deep breath.

"You won't get away with this," Ryan said. "The sheriff's department already knows you were here at this yurt, and Deni told them about seeing you near the hotel shortly before the bomb went off."

"They don't know anything," Al said. "All they have is her word, and she's a terrorist's daughter who won't be around to defend herself." He approached Mike, who stood close to Deni and Ryan, and gestured with the gun. "Kneel down."

"Make me." Mike glared at him, fists clenched at his side. "Kill me if you have to, but I'm not going to let you get away with making it look like suicide."

"I'll make you." Al turned and fired at Deni.

Time slowed down for her. She saw the muzzle of the gun pointed at her, heard the loud report, then felt a burning pain in her shoulder. "The next shot goes right in her heart if you don't do what I say," Al said.

Chapter Nineteen

Ryan felt the impact of the bullet as it pushed Deni sideways. Rage surged through him and he kicked out, striking Al hard in the back of the leg. Al staggered, and turned, the pistol leveled at Ryan, but before he could pull the trigger, Mike wrapped his arm around Al's neck and began choking him. Ryan kicked again, Al's shin hard against his heel, and the gun clattered to the floor.

"This is the sheriff!" a voice boomed. "We have you surrounded. Come out with your hands up."

"Help!" Deni screamed.

"Help!" Ryan echoed.

Scuffling noises sounded outside, and he pictured deputies swarming up the ladder. The door to the tree house burst open and the sheriff, followed by three deputies, crowded in, weapons drawn. They pointed their weapons at Mike. "Let him go," they ordered.

"Al shot me!" Deni cried. "Dad saved me!"

"Let him go," Travis ordered again.

Mike released his hold on Al, who staggered forward, clutching his throat. "He's a maniac," Al said.

"I found him up here, those two tied up, the gun in his hand. He shot his own daughter, then went after me."

"That's not what happened," Ryan said.

"Everyone quiet!" Travis ordered. "We're going to hold you both until we sort this out." He signaled to his deputies and they moved forward and put both men in handcuffs.

Gage Walker knelt next to Ryan and Deni and began cutting them free. "Travis radioed for an ambulance as soon as we heard the gunshot," he said. Together, he and Ryan eased Deni onto her back.

Ryan stripped off his jacket, then tore off his shirt and folded it into a pad and began applying pressure to her wound. "I know it hurts," he said when she cried out. "But we have to stop the bleeding." He told himself a shoulder wound wouldn't be too bad. Al hadn't meant to kill her. But if she lost enough blood it wouldn't matter what his intentions had been.

Travis knelt beside them. "The ambulance should be here soon," he said. "I need you to tell me what happened."

As concisely as he could, Ryan told about returning to the yurt to talk to Al and finding Mike in the tree house. "Al had set it up so that as soon as Mike lost his balance the table would fall over and he would strangle to death in that noose," Ryan said. "We got to him just in time. Then, when we were leaving, Al returned and ordered us up here at gunpoint. He shot Deni when Mike wouldn't kneel down so Al could shoot him. He had a suicide note he forced Mike to write so that you would all think he had shot us, then killed himself."

"I have the note in my pocket," Deni said. She was very pale, but still conscious. Ryan kept the pressure on the wound, and prayed the ambulance would hurry.

"We have security footage of a man with white hair, in a cowboy hat and Western shirt, and a fake moustache like the one Mike wore to the last town council meeting, in the courthouse a little over an hour ago," Travis said.

"It couldn't have been Mike," Ryan said. "He was here then. Al probably dressed up like that to make you think he was Mike. I think he's tried to frame Mike for all the bombings. Apparently Al was an explosives expert in the military, too. His name is Alex Coggins."

"We'll need to interview both of them," Travis said. "We'll figure out the truth."

Ryan nodded, and focused all his attention on Deni. He didn't care about Al, or Mike or anyone but her. Of all the people he had worked to rescue, none had ever meant more.

DENI WOKE TO bright light, the sensation of crisp cotton sheets and a faint beeping noise. As her vision focused, she turned to see Ryan, in a chair beside the bed. He stood and leaned over her. "Hey," he said. "How are you feeling?"

"A little foggy. And numb." The memory of everything that had happened in the tree house rushed back to her and she tried to move her left arm, but it was encased in bandages. She looked around what was clearly a hospital room. "What time is it? How long have I been here?"

"It's about seven, Thursday morning," he said. "You had surgery to remove the bullet in your shoulder. You've got some extra hardware in there now to repair some splintered bone. It will be a while before you're climbing cliffs or doing gymnastics."

"Darn. I was planning to take up both those hobbies next week."

He stroked her hair. "It's good to see you awake."

She tried to calculate how long she had been here, but her mind was still too foggy. A long time, in any case. "Have you been here the whole time?" she asked. Dark smudges shadowed his eyes and the beginnings of a beard dusted his cheeks and jaw.

"Hmmm."

She smiled, then the smile faded, replaced by a look of worry. "What happened with Dad?" She had a vague memory of a deputy putting her father in handcuffs.

"He's going to be okay. The paramedics checked him out. He had quite the ordeal, but he's already recovering. The sheriff is still holding him, but he assured me it's more protective custody."

"And Al?"

"He's in custody, too."

"I don't remember much after Al shot me," she said. "You were there, and the sheriff. What exactly happened?"

"I was so angry when Al shot you that I kicked him. And then your dad got his arm around his neck and strangled him. Then the sheriff and his deputies came in and took charge. They were apparently searching for your father when they came to the yurt, thinking they would talk to whoever was there. They heard the gunshot and rushed to the tree house."

"And they arrested my dad?"

"I guess so. I was too focused on you to pay much attention to them." He squeezed her hand gently. "Hannah, one of the search and rescue volunteers, was one of the paramedics on duty in the ambulance that came for you. She and the others took good care of you."

"You took good care of me." She tightened her hold on him.

A nurse came in and she reluctantly let go of him while the woman checked her vitals and asked about her comfort level, then checked the surgical site. As soon as the nurse left the room, the sheriff stepped in. "Hello, Deni, Ryan," he said. "The nurse said I could talk to you for a few minutes."

She tried to sit up a little straighter in bed. Ryan leaned over to adjust the pillows at her back, and worked the controls to raise the head of the bed. Travis took Ryan's place beside her. "How are you feeling?" he asked.

"I'm going to be okay," she said. "Where is my dad? Is he all right?"

"Mike is fine. He's in a cell at the sheriff's department, but at this point, it's more for his own protection." He glanced across at Ryan. "The explosives squad from Junction found the bomb at the courthouse before it went off, but by then word that a man who looked like your father had been seen placing it had already spread around town. Until the real story has time to filter out, we thought it might be a good idea to keep Mike safe.

And there's the matter of charges for the bomb he admits to having set at the Grizzly Creek bridge."

"What about Al?" she asked. "Where is he?"

"In a cell in Junction," Travis said. "He's been charged with the bombings at Caspar Canyon, the Zenith Mine, and the Nugget Hotel and the attempted bombing of the courthouse, as well as assault, kidnapping and attempted murder."

"Did you find enough evidence to convict Al?" Ryan asked. "Enough to make people believe that Deni and her father weren't involved?"

"I can't tell you everything we found," Travis said. "But when we searched his car at the yurt, we found a shirt that matched the one the suspect in the security footage from the courthouse was wearing, and the fake moustache. Al tried to say Mike had left them there, but we know from your testimony that Mike couldn't have been there. The wound on Mike's neck and tissue samples on the rope confirm that story, also."

"Was Al the person who ran us off the road?" Deni asked.

"He hasn't admitted to that," Travis said.

"He knew we were looking for Mike," Ryan said. "I think he ran us off the road to warn us off."

"Mike told us Al had explosive training from the military, too," Ryan said. "Was that true, or another of Al's lies?"

"It wasn't a lie," Travis said. "And we have other evidence that ties him to those bombs. You'll probably both be asked to testify at the trials."

"Of course," Deni said. Though the thought of reliving their ordeal in the tree house wasn't pleasant, she would do whatever was required to help put Al away for a long time. "What about agents Olivera and Ferris?"

"What about them?" Travis asked.

"Are they satisfied that Al is guilty?" she asked. "Will they leave me alone now?"

"They're the ones who tracked Al to Eagle Mountain," Travis said. "They've had him on their radar for a while, for the bombing of a dam in Ohio. They thought your father was an accomplice, but they had Al pegged as the bomber from the first."

"They never said anything!" Deni's voice shook with outrage.

"It's never a good idea to show your hand when you're dealing with criminals," Travis said.

"I wasn't a criminal, but they treated me like one," she replied.

Travis said nothing. Instead, he stepped back. "I'm glad you're doing well," he said. "Don't worry about your father. He'll be okay."

"He wouldn't say that if it was his father in jail," she observed after Travis had left.

Ryan returned to her side. "Your dad will be okay," he said. "He's tough, like his daughter."

She didn't feel like smiling, but she managed one, for his sake.

"You're tired," he said. "And I have things I need to do. I'll leave for a while, but I promise I'll be back."

"I guess I'm not going anywhere anytime soon."

He bent to kiss her on the cheek, but she turned and caught his lips. "Thank you, for everything," she whispered when the kiss ended. "I've put you through so much."

"You were worth every bit of it." Another, briefer kiss, then he was out of the room. She fell back against the pillows and closed her eyes, intending to replay his words over and over, but she was asleep almost immediately.

RYAN HAD HAD his phone on Silent while he was in the hospital. On the way to his car in the hospital lot, he pulled it out and saw that he had missed a call from his father. He hit the button to return the call.

"Hello, Ryan." His father sounded brisk and alert, what Ryan thought of as his lawyer voice, and he pictured him at his desk, in a dress shirt and tie, his suit jacket hung neatly in the closet of his office. "I have the name of that criminal lawyer you wanted."

"Thanks, Dad. Can you text me the name and number? I don't have anything to write on just now."

"Where are you?"

"I'm just leaving the hospital in Junction." He reached the truck his boss, Xander, had loaned him and hit the key fob to unlock it. "I was with Deni. She's going to be okay." He had poured out the whole story to his father around midnight last night, when he had called to ask for the name of a good criminal attorney who could represent Mike Traynor. It had been the one thing he could think of that he could do to help Deni. To his amazement his father had listened to everything without too much judgment.

"She must be a special woman, to put you to so much trouble," his dad said now.

"She is." His heart felt a little too big for his chest as he said the words.

"But her father needs a criminal attorney. Are you sure this is a good idea, son?"

"He made some bad choices, but he's not a bad guy at all," Ryan said. "He was taken in by a really bad guy."

"Like someone else we know," his father said, but there was no rancor behind the words.

"I've been staying out of trouble," Ryan said. "I learned a hard lesson, but it stuck."

"I believe you. Tell me more about Deni."

"You'd really like her. She's a schoolteacher. A good one."

"Your mother and I would love to meet her sometime."

"I'd like that, too. Maybe you could come here. There's some fly fishing streams I'd like to show you." He and his dad hadn't been fishing together in years.

It was his dad's turn to be speechless. After a moment, he said, "Maybe I could do that. We'll plan on it."

They said goodbye, but Ryan didn't start the truck right away. His dad had texted contact information for a criminal lawyer he said was one of the best, and Ryan needed to get that name and number to Mike. Would they even let Ryan in to see him? Maybe he'd have to leave a message. He should go home and take a shower, and try to get some rest, though he still felt too wired to sleep.

He started the truck. He would head toward Eagle Mountain. By the time he got there, he would have come up with a plan.

Instead of heading to the sheriff's department, Ryan made his first stop at the office of the *Eagle Mountain Examiner.* Inside, he found reporter Tammy Patterson at her desk. She looked up, frowning, then her eyes widened. "Ryan Welch, what happened to you?"

He sat in the chair in front of her desk and leaned toward her, keeping his voice low, not wanting to be overheard by the account reps and other people in the office. "Do you want an exclusive on the dramatic events that led to the arrest of the man behind the bombings that have been terrorizing the town for the last month?"

Tammy grabbed a tape recorder from the in-box at the corner of the desk. "Are you kidding? I heard they arrested some guy from out of town, but the sheriff is, as usual, being really closed-mouthed about it."

"You need to talk to Deni Traynor," Ryan said.

"Deni was involved?"

"She's the whole reason they caught the guy. He shot her and her dad got hold of him and held him until the sheriff could subdue and arrest him. She's in the hospital in Junction, but if you go up there, I'm sure she'll see you." He would call Deni and point out how a positive story in the local paper could help locals see her and her dad in a new light.

"What about you?" Tammy asked. "Were you there?"

"I was there, so I can corroborate anything Deni says, but this is her story." He stood. "You call her."

"You bet I will."

As he walked away, Tammy already had her phone in hand.

At the sheriff's department, Deputy Jake Gwynn led him downstairs, through two metal detectors to the only occupied cell in the local jail. "You have a visitor, Mike," Jake said.

Mike, dressed in plain khaki pants and shirt, stood at Ryan's approach. "Hey there," he said. "Ryan, isn't it? Have you seen Deni? Is she okay?"

"She's going to be fine. She had surgery to remove the bullet and put some pins in to stabilize some shattered bone. She's awake now and was asking about you."

"Tell her I love her. And I'm sorry. I'd give anything if none of this had happened."

"Don't worry about that now," Ryan said. "I have the name and number of a lawyer you need to call." He took out his phone and scrolled to the text his dad had sent.

"The county said they would appoint me an attorney."

"You need to call this guy. He's an expert criminal attorney out of Denver and he's agreed to defend you for a nominal fee."

Mike laughed. "And why would he do that?"

"Because he's a friend of my dad's. They went to law school together, I think. Anyway, you need to call him. For Deni's sake."

"Give the info to the deputy," Mike said. "I don't seem to have a pen on me."

Jake took the phone from Ryan. "Let me borrow this and I'll write everything down and make sure Mike gets it and makes the call."

He left them and Ryan turned to Mike. "How are you doing?" he asked.

"Better, now that I know Deni is going to be okay, and Al is locked far away from here. When I think of him shooting Deni, I see red." He shook his head. "What a mess."

"The sheriff seems pretty confident of his case," Ryan said. "And I guess there are federal charges against him, too."

"So where do you come in?" Mike said. "I never heard Deni mention you."

Ryan sucked in a deep breath. "I love your daughter," he said. "I'm planning on marrying her, if she'll have me."

"That's up to her, but I guess she could do worse." He looked Ryan up and down. "That was quick thinking, kicking Al like that. He didn't see it coming."

"There was no thinking involved," Ryan said. "It was like you said—when he shot Deni, I saw red."

"I guess that's something we have in common, then," Mike said.

Jake returned with the phone. "Here you go."

"I need to get home now," Ryan said. "Take care, Mike."

"You too, son."

Ryan walked out of the sheriff's department feeling drained. He figured he had just about enough left in him to make it back to his place before he crashed.

THE HEADLINE ON the next issue of the *Eagle Mountain Examiner* declared Father-Daughter Duo Bring Down Bomber in inch-high type across all columns. The issue appeared the day after Deni returned home. In her absence, friends had cleaned off the graffiti, and replaced it with a banner that welcomed her home.

"'Ms. Traynor had previously alerted the sheriff's office to her suspicions about Alex Coggins,'" Deni read as she sat on the sofa beside Ryan. "'Fearful for her father's safety, she and friend Ryan Welch tracked Mike Traynor to a yurt in the high country that Coggins had been using as a hideout. Coggins had kidnapped Mr. Traynor and was keeping him prisoner in a tree house behind the yurt, where Ms. Traynor and Mr. Welch found him and freed him. As they were escaping, they were intercepted by Coggins. Coggins forced Mr. Traynor at gunpoint to tie up Ms. Traynor and Mr. Welch, then shot Ms. Traynor when Mr. Traynor refused to cooperate further. Mr. Traynor was able to subdue Coggins and hold him until the sheriff's department arrived.'"

She lowered the newspaper and looked at Ryan. "She makes us all sound like heroes."

"You are a hero." He put his arm around her. "You never gave up on your father. If you hadn't kept pushing, he wouldn't be alive today."

"And I wouldn't be alive if you hadn't kicked Al." She frowned at the paper. "Tammy left out that part."

"I don't need the glory—your father does."

"Maybe not now that you have that fancy criminal attorney defending him. Dad says they're working out a plea bargain. He's hoping for probation instead of prison time."

"And no more pranks involving bombs, unarmed or otherwise."

"He's learned his lesson—I'm certain of that." She tossed the paper aside and laid her head on his shoulder. "I'm never going to forget the terrible things that happened, but I'm ready to put them behind me."

"Me, too. I think it's a good time for all of us to make a fresh start." He shifted to face her and took her hand. "Xander accepted my offer to buy an interest in the company," he said. "And I'm signing up for business courses at the community college for next semester."

"You're going to be really busy, with a new business and school and search and rescue."

He blew out a breath. "I'm taking a leave from search and rescue for a while. I probably should have done it before now. I need another surgery on my arm, and certainly I need more therapy."

"We can compare physical therapy notes," she said. She had already started rehabbing from the injury to her shoulder.

"I hope we can do more than that."

Something in his voice forced her attention back to him. "Deni, I love you," he said.

"I know that," she said. "Everything you've done has proved it. And I love you, too."

"Enough to marry me?"

She stared, unable to breathe, wondering if she had heard him correctly.

His face paled. "If it's too soon…"

"No. I mean, yes. Yes, I'll marry you. No, it isn't too soon." She reached her uninjured arm around him and hugged him close. "No way am I letting you get away now. I only wish I'd found the nerve to speak up at the coffee shop months ago. Then again, if you had known what you were in for, you might have run the other way."

"You don't see me running, do you? Except toward you."

He kissed her, and she kissed him back, until they lost track of time, and of everything but each other. As many regrets as Deni had about all that had happened, she could never be sorry that events had brought her and Ryan together. Out of all this pain had come something more wonderful than she ever could have imagined.

* * * * *

HARLEQUIN
PLUS

Announcing a **BRAND-NEW** multimedia subscription service for romance fans like you!

Read, Watch and Play.

Experience the easiest way to get the romance content you crave.

Start your **FREE 7 DAY TRIAL** at www.harlequinplus.com/freetrial.